DEAD-END
SHOOT-OUT

Weede and Kermit dropped to their knees
and aimed their pistols at the window. But
there was no target. Remington was already
loping toward the door, ejecting empty hulls,
ramming in fresh bullets from his gunbelt.
Moments later, they spotted Remington halfway down the street, stalking a man neither
of them had seen. Then the chief marshal
slipped between two buildings and disappeared.

Moments later, the crack of a rifle filled the
air. A man screamed in mortal agony, and the
two lawmen waited for the sound of Remington's .44.

But there was only silence . . .

REMINGTON #5

WYOMING BLOOD TRAIL

JAMES CALDER BOONE

AVON
PUBLISHERS OF BARD, CAMELOT, DISCUS AND FLARE BOOKS

REMINGTON #5: WYOMING BLOOD TRAIL is an original publication of Avon Books. This work has never before appeared in book form.

AVON BOOKS
A division of
The Hearst Corporation
105 Madison Avenue
New York, New York 10016

First Avon Printing: December 1987

K–R   10 9 8 7 6 5 4 3 2 1

Chapter One

The man would hang. He would drop through the trapdoor a good six feet, at a good speed. He would drop until the rope around his neck stopped him short, ten or twelve inches from the ground. If he was lucky, the heavy hangman's knot would break his miserable neck and he would die quick. If, by some chance, he survived the fall, he might die a slow, agonizing death, suffocating as he danced and dangled, scant inches from the ground. He would eventually reach the ground. In a pine box. He was guaranteed six feet of it, anyway, the sonofabitch, six feet of good Missouri soil in the Galena cemetery.

Judge Samuel Parkhurst Barnstall tried not to look at the prisoner, but the prisoner was looking at him, with soft, pleading eyes. Barnstall wondered if he was pleading for his life, or for relief from the seemingly endless courtroom procedure. A speedy trial. A fair trial. Society, as represented by the United States Government in this federal district court, guaranteed the prisoner that, too. Society, as represented by the crowd in his courtroom, wanted to see it all work, wanted to know what the prisoner had done and why he had done it and if found guilty, would want to see him hang by the neck until dead.

Barnstall did not look at the prisoner. He had looked at him all during the proceedings. He looked now at the man who held the center of attention in Barnstall's courts. He listened, too, for that was another requirement of Society, as represented by those who had written the laws and voted them into existence on behalf of the American people.

The prosecuting attorney, one Darrel LaFourche, licked dry lips, rubbed his perspiring forehead with stubby fingers. His coat hung loosely from his narrow, sloping shoulders. His trousers had lost their crease in the heat, and his string tie was rumpled from constant wadding from that same nervous hand that now tweaked his eyebrows as if his head was aching beyond human endurance.

The courtroom was nearly full, and the hot summer air moved listlessly among the spectators, many of whom flapped at their faces with paper fans. A fly buzzed near Judge Barnstall's stern face, and the bailiff leaned against the bench, his uniform stained under his arms and down his back by the sweat that oozed from his flabby pores.

"I beseech the court to find Patrick Houlihan guilty as charged in the vicious murder of Sam Nolan, guilty of stealing his money and killing Sam Nolan and drinking his ill-gotten gains before the body was cold."

LaFourche stepped away from the prosecutor's table and looked directly into the accused's eyes, then transferred his look to Barnstall. "I beg this in the name of common justice and decency on behalf of the people of the United States of America."

"Sit down, Counselor," said Barnstall, his voice booming through the courtroom. "The court finds the defendant guilty as charged."

"Oh shit," said Houlihan.

The defense attorney, Jack Kearney—like his client, an Irishman—looked at Houlihan with pity and sneaked a swig from a flask he kept in his inside coat pocket.

"Put away your whiskey, Jack," said Barnstall, "and approach the bench with your client."

Kearney coughed self-consciously, and bowed his head. He took Houlihan's arm, helped him from the chair. The two men walked toward the bench, stood at a preordained spot to await the judge's formal pronouncement.

"Patrick Houlihan," said Barnstall, "you waived a jury trial and threw yourself upon the mercy of this court. This court, however, has very little mercy for a man such as you. After listening to all the evidence in your case, and to your feeble defenses, so ably presented by your counsel, I have found you very guilty, extremely guilty, of murdering for profit a man named Sam Nolan of Hollister, Missouri. You, sir, are a drunkard and a coward, and the court has found you such.

"There is but One who can pardon your offense, but you will not meet Him in this life. Think, then, carefully, of your last moments on this good, green earth. Think long and hard of your sins and of the man you killed as you sit in your cell waiting for execution. Think long and hard of that terrible moment when you dispatched Sam Nolan's soul to his Maker, and pray that he was more prepared than you are at this very moment.

"You have two days in which to learn how to pray. I hereby sentence you to hang by the neck on Saturday morning at ten of the clock until you are dead, dead, dead!"

Houlihan's face drained of color. Jack Kearney had to hold the man up as Barnstall banged his gavel to emphasize the last three words of his unusually short speech. LaFourche, caught off guard by the abrupt end of that same speech, rose to his feet and helped Kearney hand over his client to the bailiff.

He looked up at the bench, expecting to see the imposing, black-robed figure of Judge Barnstall still sitting there. But Barnstall was gone and the courtroom spectators began to jabber until the din was like a madhouse.

"Where did he go?" asked LaFourche of the bailiff. "We've got two more cases to try this morning."

The bailiff shrugged.

"I handed him a note from one of his deputies. I don't know what it said. The judge didn't say nothin' to me. Told me to fetch Ned Remington as soon as court was adjourned."

"He didn't even adjourn the goddamned court." LaFourche squeezed sweat off his forehead and stood there, looking at the empty bench, stood stoop-shouldered and helpless as people began to file out of the courtroom, fanning themselves futilely, still buzzing at the decision of Samuel Parkhurst Barnstall, judge of the United States District Court for Southwestern Missouri in Galena.

Bucky Kermit was waiting for the judge in Barnstall's office. He wore a deputy marshal's badge on his fringed elkskin jacket. Bucky, a short, wiry man with a frazzle of curly hair under a gray felt hat with the brim pushed back flat in the front, bushy moustache drooping over thin, sensual lips, stood five foot seven and three-quarters in his boot moccasins, but he cast a long shadow over the territories where he rode for Ned Remington, Barnstall's chief deputy marshal.

Bucky carried a big bowie knife on his beaded belt, and he packed a Colt .44 with a nine-inch barrel and staghorn grips that seemed too large for his small hands. He wore the pistol low, on a gunbelt studded with cartridges, and it was tied to his leg with a leather thong. His right hand was never far from the butt of that hogleg Colt, but his crackling blue eyes gave him the appearance, always, of not having a care in the world. His slow, boyish smile, under the moustache, furthered the illusion of a carefree man who just liked to dress up in frontier clothing and play lawman.

Judge Barnstall was not fooled. He entered the room and Bucky stood up, politely.

"Bucky," said the judge.

"Judge."

"This is pretty serious."

"Yes. Mighty serious, Judge."

"Sit down, sit down." Barnstall, whose chest was twice as thick as Bucky's, his shoulders half again as broad, seemed to tower over Kermit, but in fact, he was only a few inches taller. With his bulk, his piercing blue eyes, and square, underslung chin, and dressed in a dark suit, slim, silk-string tie, and white shirt, Barnstall seemed over six feet tall, when in fact he would have to stretch a mite to reach five foot eleven. He was tall enough, and his perch on the almighty bench in Galena made him even taller.

Barnstall pulled his leather-covered chair away from the cherrywood desk and sat down, pulling the black robe over his head. He tossed it to a clothes tree and leaned over the desk, his stubby hands folded, the thumbs rotating around each other in small circles.

Barnstall's office was not large, but it suited him, his Spartan tastes. Neatly dusted lawbooks, gleaming in red, gold-embossed leather, lined the bookshelves. One wall boasted two detailed maps, one of the southwestern United States, and the other of the Indian Nations, penned on parchment. In the center of the wall hung a framed law degree from Harvard University. A large globe of the world stood on a walnut stand in one corner of the room, and beside it, a mahogany liquor cabinet on which stood a crystal decanter filled with brandy and a pair of sniffers on a porcelain tray.

The judge's desk was neatly in order, too. Papers resided in a pair of small boxes framed so that they were half a foot apart, stacked. One plaque on his desk bore his name and title, the other a legend inscribed in Latin: *Ignorantia legis neminen excusat*. Ignorance of the law is no excuse. A cigar box, also of mahogany, carved elephants and tigers on its surface, lay closed atop the desk, aromatic of fine Virginia tobacco. There was also a brass bell, highly polished, with a handle of rosewood, that the judge used to summon his clerk.

Bucky had never been in Barnstall's office before. Sitting in the oversized leather chair, the judge looked out of place and small. Yet he seemed at home, his legs crossed, a fringed sleeve draped over one arm of the chair.

"Now, tell me what happened," said Barnstall. "Spare me no details, no matter how repugnant."

Bucky didn't know what repugnant meant, but he had a pretty good idea. The other deputies talked about Barnstall a lot. They all agreed he used highfalutin' language, but they respected him. They knew that Barnstall knew what the words meant.

"Wal, sir, we was over to Springfield, layin' up last night to make an arrest early this morning. Harry Bellows, he was serving one of your warrants. Harry wanted me along because he thought the job might be more'n he could handle."

"Who was he serving?"

"Jack Cardiff. Big feller, hardrock miner from Wyoming way, mean as a bear with a thorn in its paw."

"Cardiff, Cardiff," mused Barnstall. He leafed through the papers in one of the boxes, found nothing that caught his eye. "You'll have to tell me about that one, Bucky."

"This Cardiff, according to the warrant Harry showed me, tracked this jasper Amos Washington all the way from Cheyenne, and killed him cold blood. Shoved a rifle down his throat and pulled the trigger. Made jelly soup out of his guts. Man didn't die easy, for sure."

Barnstall winced, but he had told Kermit to omit no details, gruesome or otherwise.

"Go on," he said.

"Well, when we come after Cardiff, we was jumped by a whole gang of roughs. I got knocked cold. Harry Bellows was shot the same way as that Washington feller."

"You mean Cardiff . . . ?"

"Yes sir, Judge, he plumb shoved a Sharps rifle down Harry's throat and shot a fifty-caliber ball into his belly from top to bottom. Harry didn't die right away and he was in awful agony. We got him to a barber who sawed on bones, but he couldn't do nothin'. He gave him some laudanum and Harry cried and squirmed somethin' terrible and died early this mornin'."

"That's a hellish thing for a man to do. Why?"

"I reckon this Cardiff's just one mean sonofa-bitch," said Bucky matter-of-factly.

Barnstall picked up the bell, rattled it. The clapper struck a series of melodious notes. A moment later, the clerk poked his head through the doorway.

"Where in hell's Remington?"

"He's just coming up the stairs now, your honor," said Lucius Robson, a young man in his late teens, with slicked-down hair, a lean, ascetic face, aquiline nose.

"Well, send him right in as soon as he gets here," gruffed Barnstall.

"Ned would be the man to go after Cardiff, all right," said Bucky amiably.

"You'll go, too, Bucky. You know what he looks like, where he might be."

"Oh, I expect he lit a shuck for Cheyenne after he found out Harry was a deputy marshal."

"Didn't he know that when you tried to serve the warrant?"

"Harry tried to tell him, but Cardiff and his cronies just up and started tearing assholes. I got clubbed with a rifle butt before I could say who we was. Harry, he just told Cardiff he was under arrest. We didn't show no badges when we come into the saloon."

"A saloon, was it? So, Cardiff's a drinking man." Barnstall frowned. "Liquor and guns. They're Satan's implements, Bucky."

"I reckon," said Kermit.

Both men looked up. Bucky craned his neck to see

Ned Remington stride into the room. The clerk closed the door behind him.

"What's the trouble, Sam?" asked Remington. "Howdy, Bucky, thought you was in Springfield with Harry."

"Sit down, Ned," said Barnstall. "And listen to what Bucky has to say."

Ned took the only other chair in the room, sat in it. With him in it, the chair looked small, but it was the same size as Bucky's.

Kermit told him the details of the warrant and Bellows's death. Ned listened with sober attention, saying nothing until the deputy marshal was finished with his account.

Barnstall continued to look through the papers on his desk. Finally, he pulled out a copy of a warrant, read it through. His blue eyes crackled as he recalled something he had forgotten.

"I remember this case now," said Barnstall. "Harry and I discussed the warrant before he accepted the assignment to serve it. He had run across Cardiff before. Harry thought there was more to the case than simple murder, Ned. I should have listened more carefully to him. Harry was a wise old bird."

"I know," said Ned cryptically.

"I picked Harry for this assignment because he had done some work up in Cheyenne for me some time back."

"I remember," said Ned. "Rustlers, wasn't it?"

"Yes. Harry did well, but he was never satisified that he had finished the job—even though he brought in three men who were subsequently tried, convicted and sentenced—to hang."

"Harry was a peculiar sort," said Bucky. "Never said a whole hell of a lot, but when he did, it was pretty damned important. He told me Cardiff was going to be either real easy or real hard. I never could make sense of it until I saw the man. He looked like he was carved out of a chunk of iron and tempered in hellfire."

"The bigger they are . . ." said Barnstall.

"That's what Harry used to say," said Remington.

Barnstall laughed. Bucky looked at the two men, saw that they were mourning Harry in their own ways.

"One time I sent Harry into the Nations after a kid we wanted to try for robbery," said Sam. "I gave Harry the warrant and he rode off, saying he wouldn't need any help. After all, it was just a kid, he said. Well, Harry came riding back to Galena without the kid. He didn't even have the warrant. I asked him what happened. 'Judge,' he said, 'I found the kid, showed him the warrant. He showed me the business end of a double-barreled shotgun. Told me to eat that paper warrant and get my ass out of there.'

"I was dumbfounded. I asked Harry what he did then. 'Hell, I ate every piece of that warrant. Chewed it up, swallered it. I'm here and I'm alive, ain't I?'"

Ned and Bucky roared with laughter.

"There was the time," said Remington, "when Harry was trying to serve a warrant down Texas way in one of those Red River saloons. I was sitting at the bar, trying to act like wallpaper, and Harry was sitting at a back table, watching the door. He got an itch in his foot and leaned over to take his boot off. When he looked up, there were the four men we had come hunting. They stood over him, ready to slap leather.

"I was about to bail Harry out, when he sat back up and his hand was already filled. He pointed his Colt at the four hardcases cool as could be. 'Boys,' he said, 'there's six bullets in here, and four of you. Somebody's gonna get killed twice.'"

Barnstall and Kermit doubled up with laughter. Ned joined in, and when they finally stopped, there were tears in their eyes.

"Ned," said the judge, "I want you and Bucky to go after Jack Cardiff. I'll make out a new warrant charging him in the murder of a federal officer. Lucius will have the papers ready by this afternoon."

Remington and Bucky exchanged glances.

"I want to take Jimson Weede on this one, Sam," said Remington.

"Fine with me, Ned. May I ask why?"

"That partner of Cardiff's was a colored man."

"I didn't know that," said Barnstall.

"Harry Bellows did. He told me something I'll never forget before he and Bucky went out to serve that warrant. He said, 'Bad enough to kill a man in anger for monetary gain, but to make a man kneel, beg for his life, then call him a nigger and make him swallow a fifty-caliber Sharps is just plain mean. Better to hit a child in anger, than strike him in cold blood.'"

"So, you know how Amos Washington died," said Barnstall.

"Yeah, but not how Harry died until Bucky told me," said Remington grimly. "Seems to me Cardiff's about as nasty as they come."

"I want him brought in alive, Ned," said the judge.

"We'll do our best."

"Fine. I want you to go to Cheyenne, contact the territorial marshal there." Barnstall rifled through some papers, came up with the one he needed. "Owen Carberry. Know him?"

"No," said Remington. He looked at Bucky. Bucky shook his head.

"See if he will help you. Take the Union Pacific out, rent horses when you get there. I'll advance expenses."

"You'll advance money?" Ned asked. "That's a surprise."

Barnstall coughed.

"Well, this is a special case. I want Harry Bellows's killer in my court. And, there's something else, too."

"What's that?" asked Remington.

"Harry thought there was more to the Washington case than simple murder. I should have listened to him. Harry was a wise old bird."

"I know," said Remington, thoughtfully. "If Harry thought there was more to it, there was more to it. Bucky, he say anything to you about it?"

"Maybe. He said a man don't kill like Cardiff did unless he's got a powerful hate in him. And he said that maybe Cardiff was trying to send a message to someone else."

Remington stood up. He towered over Barnstall and Kermit. Bucky got up too.

"That's it, then," said Ned. "We'll do some looking in Cheyenne, see if we can't find out who Cardiff was trying to reach."

"Ned, you just bring Cardiff in. Let the territorial marshal worry about why he killed Washington."

"See you later, Sam," said Ned, stalking out of the room. Bucky looked at Barnstall, shrugged, and followed in Remington's footsteps.

Barnstall looked down at the papers on his desk, frowned.

Chapter Two

Jimson Weede swung the axe over his head, slammed it downward with powerful force. The axe struck the chunk of hickory and split it in two, thwacked into the oak stump a full two inches. The kindling fell to the ground. Weede worked the axe loose, set another two foot wedge of hickory atop the stump. Shirtless, his ebony skin glistened with a sheen of sweat as the fiery sun beat down from the clear, cloudless Missouri sky.

The black man looked at his mixed-breed beagle hound lying on the porch with its eyes closed, its head resting on its folded paws. The hound lifted its head, cocked it slightly. Weede dropped to one knee, put his ear to the ground. Seconds later, the hound leaped from the porch, raced off down the road, through the woods, barking at whoever was riding toward the cabin.

Weede's old Colt hung in its holster from a ten-penny nail driven into one of the corner posts of the porch. Jim looked at it, measured the distance. He lifted the axe, swung it downward with great force. The wooden *plunk* of the blade as it split the hickory sounded almost musical. The hound continued to bark for several seconds, then stopped. Weede smiled.

He was born in 1847 of a runaway Negro slave who lived with a Creek woman, was captured by a group of slave traders ten years later on the docks at Savannah and sold to a man who took the boy to Texas, gave him his name as a joke. He taught Weede to ride a horse and shoot both pistol and rifle. The man moved to St. Louis, then to Springdale, Arkansas. When the war broke out, his master moved up to Rolla, Missouri, joined the Union forces. He came back once, in 1863, to give Weede his freedom, then rejoined his regiment. He also gave Weede a thirty-one–caliber Colt Navy and a Harper's Ferry musket. Then he drowned crossing the White River during a spring flood, and a man came to the house one day and ran Weede off the property. Jim drifted south, lived in abandoned farms until the war ended. During the Reconstruction, he hunted and fished, sold the meat to new settlers in the White River Valley. When Ned Remington met him and learned of his background, he told Weede that since he had been born and raised in the Nations, he was considered a Creek by law. When Remington saw how Weede handled a gun, he offered him a job as a deputy U.S. marshal. Weede was as proud of his badge as he was of his Colt .45 and his Henry .44, kept it polished and shined.

He heard the approaching hoofbeats clearly now, and the squawk of a jay, the jiggling petals of a flowering dogwood down the road, confirmed the approach of someone who was most likely a friend. Jim buried the axe-blade in the chopping block and walked to the porch. He leaned against the post where his pistol hung and waited.

Bucky Kermit rode into the clearing, his floppy hat shading his face. But Weede noticed that his saddle-horn was dripping with holsters, pistol butts jutting from the leather. Bucky rode a short-legged buckskin pony, not a fancy horse but one, Weede knew, that could live on native grass for long stretches of time.

"Bucky," said Weede.

"Evenin', Jim."

"Set down. I got terbaccy, some cider cool in a clay jug."

Bucky swung out of the saddle and Weede saw the fifty-caliber Sharps carbine like a giant fin in its boot. Bucky's saddlebags bulged, and his bedroll was thonged behind the cantle, wrapped in a dark slicker. Kermit stuck a matchstick between his teeth, walked bowlegged over to the porch steps. He did not sit down, but put one moccasined boot on the lowest board. He pushed on it.

"Ought to tighten that board up, Jim."

"No sir, Bucky," he drawled, "that's the first thing I hear when someone creepin' up on me."

Bucky laughed.

"You want somethin', Bucky, or you just want to go 'roun' my house checkin' for loose boards?"

"Ned wants you and me to ride a train up to Cheyenne with him. He's pickin' up warrants this afternoon."

"Who we after?" asked Weede, his mahogany face expressionless.

"Feller name of Cardiff. Jack Cardiff."

Weede scowled. He flashed white teeth, but it was not a smile.

"He the one what . . .?"

"He's the one," said Bucky. "Now, he's gone and kilt Harry Bellows."

Weede let out a low whistle of surprise through suddenly puckered lips. He jerked away from the post, stood square on his feet. At five foot nine, he was slightly taller than Bucky, but he seemed larger. The veins stood out on the muscles of his arms, and his skin was smooth, like polished ebony.

Weede knew that a man named Cardiff had tracked a black man all the way from Cheyenne to Springfield and had shot him in cold blood. At the time, he had not thought too much about it, except to wonder why a white man would go so far to kill a black. He had asked no questions, but figured Harry Bellows would bring Cardiff in and that would be the end of it. Harry had done such many times before.

"How could Cardiff kill a man like Harry Bellows?" asked Weede.

"He had help," said Bucky.

"You was with him." A flat statement. Toneless, without any accusatory inflection.

"I was out cold when it happened. There was witnesses saw it happen. Same as with Amos Washington."

"That the black man Cardiff killed?"

"Yeah. We gotta ride, Jim, you want to saddle up. We'll stable the horses in Springfield, catch the train up to Kansas City and head west."

"Won't take but a minute."

"What about that hound dog, what's his name?"

"I calls him Skittles. He'll live on squirrel and field mice, get water from the branch."

"I'll help you shut up things here."

"Much obliged, Bucky." Weede climbed the porch, grabbed the door to open it. He stopped, looked back at Kermit. "Why you reckon Remington wants me along?" he asked. "'Cause I'm a black man?"

"I thought you was Creek blood," said Kermit evenly.

Weede laughed, and it was a rare enough thing that Bucky stood there dumbfounded for a long moment, trying to swallow his surprise.

Ned Remington used the key taken from Harry Bellows's effects and opened the door to his small house in the woods near Reeds Spring, Missouri, not far from Galena. The house was empty, quiet, as the tall man entered. He surveyed the dim front room with narrowed, iron-gray eyes. He rubbed a thumb across the blue stubble that shadowed his chin and closed the door. He opened a curtain and a shaft of light illuminated the room. Dust motes danced and sparkled in the stirred-up air.

He looked at the small rock fireplace, the clean-swept hearth, the mantle. A Kentucky rifle, passed down to Harry by his father, hung above the mantle, long and sleek, the barrel browned, the wood polished. A powder horn hung from a nail alongside. Ned knew there was a new flint, bound with a small square of leather, screwed to the lock, and he knew where Harry kept the round brass patchbox with a compartment for extra flints. He felt a twinge of sadness as he looked at the chair that Harry had made of willow saplings and cowhide, the divan that he had hauled down from Springfield—bought from a family down on their luck, who were returning east where life was not so harsh—and the table Harry had carried all the way from Kansas City on horseback because it had drawers that locked and was made in China. The table looked out of place in the room, with its shiny black paint, its red and yellow dragons.

Ned went to the corner of the big woven rug and

pulled it back. There was the key to the desk drawers. He stooped and picked it up, walked to the table. He opened the left drawer and then, with the same key, the right. He sat down on the chair made from a nail keg, upholstered with buckskin and cotton batting. That, too, Harry had made, and it wasn't very comfortable, just serviceable, because Harry said he didn't want to spend a lot of time at his "desk." It was another of Harry's jokes, but Ned knew that the deputy did spend time there, thinking and jotting down notes, writing out his reports and expense accounts to turn over to Judge Barnstall's court at Galena after completion of his lawman's duties in the territories.

Ned dug through the papers, found the little book he was looking for. It was like a diary, with red and black leather for a binding, but it had no dates in it. Rather, it had sleeves where papers could be placed. When one book was full, it could be removed and put away and another inserted in its place. Ned hoped that the book inside was not empty, because he did not know where Harry kept his papers over the years. He thought he sent them to a sister up in Nebraska, but he wasn't sure.

He opened the book. It had a date on the first page. There was another date on the next page, and the notation: "Cheyene." Ned laughed at Harry's spelling, but this was what he had hoped to find. He leafed through the book quickly, saw that it contained several pages of notes, all pertaining to his investigation of the Cattleman's Association in Cheyenne the previous year.

One name appeared more than any other. Remington read the report quickly, went back over it again. On the surface, there was nothing incriminating, nothing solid he could hold up to the light. Only that

one name. Again, Harry misspelled it: "Carbery."
That would be Owen Carberry, the territorial marshal
in Cheyenne, unless Ned missed his guess. On another page, he saw the initial *O* before the name and
felt a sense of relief.

There were notations indicating the names of
ranchers that Harry had interviewed. Packer, Delaney, Banse, Morriss, Phipps, Stucker. On one page,
he read the notation: "Rustlers gone. No arrests. J.
Cardif had bill of sale for cattle. Bought from Faron.
Case closed. Maybe."

That "Maybe" bothered Remington. Harry didn't
like loose ends. He had come back from Cheyenne
and the head of the Cattleman's Association had sent
a letter to Judge Barnstall commending Bellows for
his work. When Sam read it to Harry, Bellows
snorted and laughed out loud. Ned tried to remember
what Harry had said at that time. "Every trail I followed," he had said, "closed up tighter'n a pawn-
broker's fist. Records were altered, or disappeared.
People who had lost stock suddenly said they had
been mistaken. I think there's a ring there in
Cheyenne, but I couldn't find no way to crack it."

A ring. For Harry to say such a thing meant he had
a pretty strong hunch. But Barnstall said that as long
as there were no further complaints, and in light of
the letter from Jerome Lundeen, head of the Cattleman's Association, the case was indeed closed.

Maybe, thought Remington.

Ned skipped ahead in the book, flipping the pages
quickly to see where Harry had left off. He found a
notation on the page following the report that brought
him up straight in the chair. Ned read it, as the
hackles rose on the back of his neck.

Ned, if you're reading this then I must be dead. And, if I was killed by someone from Cheyene, then you got to go back there and start looking for Jack Cardif and find out who he works for. More I think about it, the more I think the CA laid down some blind trails for me. I know, they were the complainers, but that only makes me more suspicious. Maybe they wanted to draw atention away from theirselves. Maybe I found something back there and didn't know what it meant at the time. You look at my book real close, see was there something I missed. I think Carbery knows something he aint teling.

Remington looked through the other papers in both drawers, but could find nothing pertinent to either the CA or the Cardiff case. He closed and locked the drawers, kept the daybook. He put the key back under the rug. He walked through the house, looked into Harry's bedroom with its single bunk, a wardrobe with a few pants and shirts hanging from nails. There were two pairs of boots by the bunk, a rifle hanging on a pair of cow horns attached to the wall. The kitchen was just as spare as the other rooms. There were pots and pans, a woodstove on which to cook, a teakettle. Coffee, sugar, and flower tins stood on a rickety counter. The table was clean, but bore whiskey bottles, a glass that smelled of Old Overholt. There was a clay ashtray, a crumpled sack of Bull Durham, a packet of cigarette papers, a box of sulphur matches.

Harry hadn't left much, Ned thought. He had lived neat and spare. From the looks of his bunk, made up neat, he had slept nights, with a clear conscience. That was more than most men could say.

Remington poured a half a tumbler of whiskey, drank it down.

"Good-bye, Harry," he said, his eyes watering.

He stalked from the house, locked the front door, and caught up his horse. He stuck the daybook in his saddlebag and rode the trail back to Galena, following the contours of the Ozark hills, seeing the tracks of deer, smelling bear scat at one place, and flushing a covey of quail out of a thicket just above a deep hollow.

There wasn't a lot to go on from what he had read of Harry's notes, but the very fact that Bellows had been suspicious was enough to make Ned want to check into Carberry and the Cattleman's Association a little more thoroughly once they got to Cheyenne.

Maybe there was a connection between Cardiff and the CA, or Cardiff and Carberry. One thing was sure. Harry Bellows was dead, and a man from Cheyenne had killed him. And why had Amos Washington been murdered in the first place? And so brutally?

If Washington had run away from something, why not just let him be? Springfield was a long way from Cheyenne. No, Washington had been a threat. He had been important enough that Cardiff had tracked the man to Missouri and then killed him in cold blood.

Ned knew he would need all of his wits to find the answers to his questions. It was no longer a simple matter of picking up a man wanted for murder and bringing him back to Judge Barnstall's court to stand trial.

No, he had to find out why Harry Bellows had been killed in the same way as an obscure Negro man named Amos Washington, and in virtually the same place. Fate? Coincidence? Remington thought there was a great deal more to this case than met the eye.

And he was determined to find the answers.

"Harry," he said aloud, "if only you could talk."

He looked back, then, at the saddlebag and smiled. Maybe Harry could talk, if not in person, then from the grave.

Chapter Three

Bucky Kermit looked into the steel-gray eyes of Ned Remington and knew the man was deadly serious.

"You want to know the names of those other jaspers who jumped me when Cardiff killed Harry?"

"That's right," said Ned. "Ever seen 'em before? Were they Missouri men or did they come down from Cheyenne with Cardiff?"

"They weren't from Cheyenne, I know that. Hell, Ned, I don't know who they were. They looked like local sodbusters. I think that's how come they got the jump on me so quick. Just ordinary jaspers. Like you see ever' day. Never saw 'em before, probably never see 'em again."

"Then we're going back to that saloon and find out who knows what."

"Judge Barnstall know about this?"

"Shut up, Bucky," said Remington amiably. "Sometimes you talk too damned much."

"I'm ready to go, then."

"Get Weede and I'll draw our advances. Meet you in front of the courthouse."

"Weede's over to McGill's Dry Goods buying a shirt."

"Give me ten minutes."

The two men stood in Remington's small office, two blocks away from the town square. Here was where Ned kept his wanted posters, records, files, supplies that could be gathered at a moment's notice. There was a bench, which served as a waiting room, but was actually part of the one-room office, a desk, three chairs, a gun cabinet that was kept locked, one window that looked out on the street. There were wall maps and a calendar. In one corner stood a folding cot that made into a bunk when Ned or a deputy on duty needed sleep. The front window was grimy, and the lettering, in black, and simply: U.S. Marshal's Office.

Bucky touched a finger to his hatbrim, opened the gate in the railing that separated the "waiting room" from the rest of Ned's office. He left the front door ajar as he stepped onto the street. He walked down, peered inside McGill's, saw that Weede was still inside. Kermit leaned against the false front, dug out the makings. He rolled a quirly, struck a sulphur match, touched it to the twisted end, sucked deeply. Smoke scratched at his lungs as he drew the smoke in, held it for a moment to savor the pungent aroma. He thought about it all over again, as he had ever since he came to in time to see Cardiff ram a rifle barrel down Harry's throat and pull the trigger. He could still see Harry's body jerk as the lead ball tore through his flesh, ripped into bone and vital organs. The explosion tore out his throat, ruptured arteries. Blood fountained out of the gaping wound as Harry's eyes glazed over in that final frost of death.

Bucky shuddered at the remembrance of that moment. But he thought back, now, to those moments before the shooting, when he had gone with Harry to find the Springfield bar reputed to be the place where Bellows might find Jack Cardiff.

"There gonna be any trouble with Cardiff?" Bucky had asked. Harry had been riding a strawberry roan that day, and when he spat his tobacco juice, he added to the freckles on the horse's shoulder.

"Not if he comes peaceably," said Harry.

"You think he will?"

"Not likely."

The saloon was on Jefferson Street, near St. Louis. It was called Monty's Saloon & Card House. It had a dirt floor covered with sawdust, a long bar made out of pine. There were tables, chairs, spittoons, a wooden rail a man could rest his boots on, lanterns for lamps, and bawdy posters on its walls. It was cool inside; smelled of beer, whiskey, cigar and cigarette smoke. At that hour of the day, just before noon, there was only one card game; two or three other men were sitting at tables, and two men sat at the bar, as if they had been there ever since it opened.

Harry had taken a chair at a table. Bucky sat at the bar, on a stool nearest the Dutch doors. The top door was swung open, the bottom, shut. Light streamed through the windows and doors, danced with the stirred-up motes of sawdust. Harry ordered the bar whiskey and Bucky asked for a pail of beer, two boiled eggs.

From his perch on the barstool, Bucky could see their horses tied to the hitchrail outside. His steel-dust gray was switching its tail, standing hipshot in the shade of the false front. The roan was shaking flies off its neck, tossing its head and mane, snorting. Bucky sipped his beer. It was cool, tasted faintly of baked clay. He supposed they cooled it in *ollas*, like the Mexicans, kept it in a dark room with wet cheese-cloth over the opening of the jug.

Harry didn't touch his whiskey, but moved the glass between his fingers, rotating it with maddening slowness. Harry's eyes flickered as men came and went through the Dutch door. Bucky was halfway through the pail when a giant man's frame filled the open half of the doorway. The man carried a big rifle in his hands. It looked like a toy in those huge hands. Bucky looked at Harry. Harry nodded.

The other three men came in through the back. Bucky didn't see them until they were right on top of him. One was short, with a scraggly beard, bright, close-set eyes so pale they were almost colorless. The other two looked like brothers, dark-complexioned, smooth-faced, oily, wearing battered felt hats, guns tucked into their waistbands. They grabbed Bucky as he came off his stool. Cardiff threw down on Harry. The short man brought his pistol up like a club and struck Bucky in the temple. That was the last thing he remembered before they brought him back to con-sciousness. The two big men had his arms pinned behind him. The short man held his pistol to Harry's throat.

Cardiff stood over Bellows, cocked the rifle, rammed it down his throat. Bucky winced, heard the explosion, saw Harry jerk and his throat open up, spew forth blood.

Then, Cardiff had turned, looked at Bucky.

"Tell 'em not to come after me no more," he said. One of the men holding him pulled out Bucky's own pistol and clubbed him senseless with it. Bucky woke up in the barber shop with a knot on his skull.

It was funny, he thought. He hadn't remembered Cardiff saying anything to him until just that moment.

He had blocked it out, or maybe the blows on the head had scrambled his memory. But he remembered it all, now, and the way Cardiff had looked at him, what he had said.

Weede strode out of the dry-goods store, walked over to Bucky.

"I'm ready," he said.

"We're riding to Springfield," said Bucky. "We'll meet Ned at the courthouse, I reckon."

"Anything else?"

"We're stopping off at the cardhouse before we catch that train to Cheyenne," Bucky said.

Weede's eyes widened slightly, but he said nothing. The two men walked to their horses, hitched at a rail down the street. Weede put his goods in his saddlebags and the two rode down to the square to wait for Remington.

Ned took the voucher from Lucius Robson, looked it over. His eyebrows lifted somewhat.

"The judge wants you to spare no expense on this one," said the clerk.

"I reckon," said Remington. "He say why?"

"He said something about how it was for Harry Bellows."

"I didn't know the judge was sentimental."

"He isn't. He said he wanted to see that bastard Cardiff hang from the gallows out there on the square."

"Yeah, he would," said Remington. "I'll be seeing you, Robson."

"The judge told me to tell you one more thing."

"And?"

"You're to go straight to Cheyenne. No place else."

"What is he? A mind reader?"

Lucius laughed.

"Mr. Remington, you know I think he is. I really do."

"So do I," growled Remington as he left the office. He walked down the stairs, crossed the square to the Stone County Bank and presented the voucher to the teller. The teller looked at him, then at the signature and shrugged. Remington suppressed a smile.

When he emerged from the bank, he saw Bucky and Weede ride up. He nodded to them, stuffed the bills in his pocket. He mounted his horse and fell in beside them.

"Everything okay?" asked Bucky, looking at Remington.

Remington glanced up at the window where Judge Barnstall often stood looking out when he was not on the bench. He was not there.

"Everything's just fine," Ned told him.

That's when Bucky started to worry.

The three lawmen rode into Springfield over the Boston Road, arrived at dusk. Bucky was all for putting up at a hotel, but Remington wanted to go to the saloon first. Weede never said a word, but he checked the action of his pistol, spun the cylinder, and put the hammer on half-cock.

"We'll just ask a few questions," said Remington.

"I'm just gettin' ready for the replies," countered Weede.

They tied their horses a few doors down from the saloon, walked toward the glow of light that illuminated the street in front of the card house. Remington went in first, followed by Bucky and Jim. The saloon was crowded, with men lining the bar, occupying the card tables. The noise of conversation mingled with the swick of cards, the click of chips, the scrape of chairs, clink of glasses. A blue pall of smoke hovered just under the hanging lanterns.

"Look real close, Bucky," said Remington, under his breath. "You give me the high sign if you see any familiar faces."

The three men stood just inside the door, surveying the room. Their marshal's badges gleamed in the light. Men looked up from their drinks and card hands. Most of them lowered their gaze and went back to their prime interests, but one table's inhabitants did not look away.

"Those look like the men who helped Cardiff out," said Bucky, nodding to the table in the far corner.

"Sure?"

"See that little one. He's either him or a twin."

"How about the other two?"

"They look like brothers to you? Them's the ones."

"Spread out," said Ned, "not too far apart."

The three marshals strode to the far table. Some men scooted their chairs out of the way. Weede flanked Remington on the chief marshal's left, Kermit held the right flank. Weede covered the men at the bar, watching them from the corner of his eye.

Remington stopped at the table. The conversations died away. A silence filled the saloon. Bucky and Jim drifted off to the side, effectively bracing the three men seated at the table.

"Marshal?" said the small man. "Somethin' you wanted?"

"Your name, for one thing."

"Why, folks here call me Leland. Leland Stuckey."

"And you two?" Remington fixed his gaze on the two taller men.

"I'm Clay Wyman. This is my brother, Rick."

So the two were brothers, thought Ned. Stuckey had one of his hands under the table. The Wyman brothers had both hands in sight.

"What can we do for you, Marshal?" asked Stuckey.

"You can tell me what you know about a man named Jack Cardiff," said Remington.

Sometimes a man's eyes shadow the future. Sometimes, the lids come down and hide the intent in a man's heart. And, sometimes, a man's eyes just look like a dark alley, a place where you can't see any shapes or figures, but only sense that something is down there, something crawling with vermin and snarling with hunger, flashing sharp teeth and lurking with eyes that glitter like broken glass.

Remington looked into Stuckey's eyes and saw these things, in an instant, and he saw, too, in Stuckey's eyes, the cold glint of a Montana morning in winter, the chilling emptiness of a snake's impersonal gaze on its prey.

Remington also sensed the other two hardcases stiffening, and he heard Weede's hand brush against the leather of his holster. Kermit shifted the weight on his feet, started to go into a crouch.

"When you bring that hand up from under the table, it better be empty," said Remington evenly. His gaze locked on Stuckey's and it seemed that an invisible wire stretched between the two men, tautened to the point of snapping.

"You don't scare me, Marshal," said Stuckey, but he licked dry lips and he swallowed hard.

"You've got about three seconds to show that other hand, Stuckey, or I'll open the ball."

Stuckey looked at the two Wyman brothers. Rick

moved his head to one side, almost imperceptibly. Clay's eyelashes flapped in a sudden blink.

The table came up off its legs, hurtled toward Remington as Stuckey kicked it away. Remington dove sideways, clawing for his pistol. Weede's hand clasped his gunbutt and Kermit went the rest of the way into his crouch, hand streaking for his sidearm.

Stuckey brought the sawed-off shotgun up level and hammered back both barrels. He squeezed off a shot that ripped through the top edge of the table and scattered double-ought buckshot in a wide deadly spray. A lantern shattered, flinging gobs of hot oil in all directions. Men screamed, and two pellets struck a cardplayer in the temple. He crumpled in his chair like a pole-axed steer, hit the floor with a dull thud. Men scattered like prairie chickens in a hail storm.

Remington hit the floor, rolled as he drew his .44, swung it on Stuckey. Stuckey saw the movement, brought the shotgun down in a new aiming position. Remington cocked his pistol, squeezed the trigger. It happened so fast, a series of small actions that smoothed together in a single flow, that Stuckey had no chance to pull the other trigger. Remington's pistol exploded, bucked in his hand. The barrel spewed out smoke and orange flame, spit a lead ball into Stuckey's throat. The force of the ball drove him backwards. The scattergun rose up in the air as Stuckey squeezed the trigger. He blew a chunk out of the ceiling and fragments of splintered wood rained down in a cloud of choking dust. Blood spurted from the hole in Stuckey's throat as he hit the wall. A fist-sized rupture in his back smeared blood four inches wide in a streak as the outlaw slid downward to a sitting position. He gasped for breath and his lips turned a cyanean blue.

Clay Wyman fired a wild shot that plowed a furrow in one wall, splatted through a windowpane, blasted glass splinters onto the street. Rick Wyman fired two quick shots at Weede before the black man put a bullet into Wyman's side, just below the rib cage. Rick dropped his pistol and sagged against the overturned table. Bucky shot Clay twice, in the arm and leg, before Clay dropped his pistol and threw up his hands in surrender.

Remington grabbed a table leg and jerked it out of the way. He leveled his pistol at Clay.

"I'll give you the same three seconds I gave Stuckey," said the lawman. "I want to know about Jack Cardiff, pronto."

Clay looked at his brother, who lay doubled up on the floor, blood pooling up in the sawdust from the wound in his side. Rick's face was contorted in pain, wrinkled up with the agony of internal injuries.

"Cardiff, why he . . ."

A rifle shot sounded from outside the saloon. The front window exploded as the bullet tore through, smashed Clay in the forehead. He was dead before he hit the ground.

Remington spun around, looked through the cloud of smoke.

He saw the big man level the rifle again and fire at Rick. Rick gave a grunt as the bullet burrowed into his skull, exploded it to shredded pulp. Brain matter, blood, and oily fluids spattered those nearby. Rick slumped over, as dead as his brother.

Remington ducked, tried to see through the smoke. The big man at the window fired off another round, then leaped away as Remington fired a shot through the front window. Glass sprayed outward as the pane disintegrated under the impact of the forty-four slug.

Weede and Kermit dropped to their knees, aimed their pistols at the window.

But there was no target.

"Who was that?" asked Weede.

Remington was already loping toward the door, ejecting empty hulls, ramming in fresh bullets from his gunbelt.

"Did you see him?" Bucky asked Weede.

Weede shook his head.

"Ned?" shouted Weede.

Remington glanced backward before he disappeared through the door.

"Come on," he said, "it's Jack Cardiff out there."

Jimson and Bucky lurched to their feet and broke into a run. Men cleared a path for the two lawmen.

Smoke hung in the air like a fog and three men lay dead on the sawdust floor of the saloon. Two of them were killed by a man named Jack Cardiff, whose marksmanship was as keen as his nerve.

"I thought you said Cardiff went back to Cheyenne," said Weede as they cleared the door and hit the street.

"I sure as hell thought he lit a shuck," said Bucky.

"Well, he sure got back here fast," cracked Weede.

They saw Remington, a shadow in the growing darkness, halfway down the street, stalking a man neither of them had seen. The chief marshal slipped between two buildings.

A moment later, they heard the crack of a rifle.

A man screamed in mortal agony and the two lawmen waited for the sound of Remington's .44.

But there was only silence.

The night seemed to get darker as the two men crouched and edged toward the last place they had seen Remington alive, their pistols held high, fingers on the triggers.

Chapter Four

Jimson Weede was the first to reach the narrow passageway between the saddlery store and the haberdasher's. He peered into the shadowy darkness.

"See anything, Jim?" asked Bucky in a low whisper.

"Not a damned thing. I'll go low, you stay high. Check our rear as we go."

"Right," said Bucky.

Weede hunched over, moved down the passageway. Bucky stood straight, followed him. He glanced back over his shoulder every so often to see if anyone came around behind them.

It was a hell of a place for an ambush, Bucky thought. Maybe that's what had happened to Ned. Maybe Cardiff had just waited for him in the alley and shot him when he came out from between the two buildings. He felt a sudden wave of suffocation grip him in the darkness. It was like walking through a dark tunnel, into a tomb.

Weede inched ahead slowly. He walked like a hunchback, for all his size, and he made no sound. Bucky looked back, then ahead, his finger caressing the trigger of his pistol. The claustrophobia became more intense, and he felt the sweat break out on his forehead, felt his palms go clammy, slick. A man with a rifle could keep them at bay, shoot them like fish in a barrel, he thought.

"See anything, Jim?" he croaked.

"Shhh."

Iron bands tightened around his chest. Weede moved so slowly and he was so quiet the silence hurt Bucky's ears. He stepped carefully right behind the black man, and his nerves began to twang. Somewhere ahead, in the alley behind the buildings, he heard a man groan.

Weede stopped. Bucky bumped into him, pulled away, tense with anticipation.

"What was that?" Bucky whispered.

"I don't know," said Weede. "Somebody's hurt, I think."

"Let's go on."

"Yeah," said Weede, and moved slowly forward. The alley, slightly brighter in the darkness of the passageway, loomed ahead. Bucky felt a loosening of the bands around his chest, but he still breathed hard, as if he were in a closet and someone were sucking the air out of it.

Weede came to the alley, halted. He poked his head around the corner of the saddlery building. He looked both ways. The alley was faintly lit by the few stars overhead. Again, they heard a man groan, off to the left.

"See anything?" whispered Bucky.

"I—I think so," said Weede. He stood up, plastered himself to the building and moved along it. Bucky followed. He saw the darker hump growing out of the ground. His heart sank. The man groaned again.

Weede got to him first. He stooped, bent over him.

"Is it Ned?" asked Bucky.

"I don't know."

Weede brought his head down, close to the wounded man's. He looked intently at the man's features, touched the man's cheek.

"No, it's not Ned," he told Bucky.

"Who is it?"

"I don't know. He's in a bad way. I think he's got a chest wound."

Bucky squatted beside Weede and the downed man. He looked all around, then he touched the man's chest. His hand came away sticky with blood. The man groaned. He was big, wide-shouldered.

"We'll get you a doctor," said Weede, leaning down close to the man.

"He won't make it," said Bucky, sliding his hand under the man's back. There was so much blood he knew the man had not long to live. There was a hole in his back he could barely cover with his hand. He swore softly.

They heard the footsteps then, and both lawmen braced themselves, brought their pistols up.

A man's form loomed out of the pewtered darkness and the lawmen relaxed. Weede stood up.

"What happened, Ned?" he asked.

Ned Remington stopped in their midst, looked down at the dying man.

"Cardiff was waiting for me. This man came out of the back door of the saddlery, started toward me. Cardiff shot him in cold blood."

"Cardiff got away," Bucky said, pulling himself to his feet. It was a flat statement.

"He had a horse tied down at the end of the alley. I didn't have a chance for a shot. I did what I could for this man, but I think . . ."

They heard the man choke, then a rattle sounded in his throat. He shuddered and let out his last gasp. He did not breathe back in again.

"His name was Willard," said Remington. "He had no connection with Cardiff."

"So, now what do we do?" asked Weede.

"We'll have to hunt Cardiff down," said Remington. "I'm surprised he's still in Missouri."

"Looks like he meant to kill those boys all along," said Bucky.

"I thought about that," Ned replied. "He could have shot us just as easily."

"More easily," said Weede. "We had our backs to him."

"I know," said Remington. "Let's see what we can find out back at the saloon. Somebody should know about Willard."

"You think Cardiff will come back?" asked Bucky.

"Not likely. I think he got what he came after. I expect he'll go back to Wyoming Territory now. Nothing I know of to keep him here."

"Train?" Bucky reloaded his pistol in the dark, by feel.

"Yeah," said Remington. "Unless he's in no hurry."

"You think he is," said Weede.

"I think he is," said Remington.

The bartender poured drinks, set out bottles along the bar as men lined up. They peered at the dead men, and some spoke of the battle they had seen. The hubbub made a din that carried up and down the street. When the three lawmen walked back in the saloon, the patrons looked at them and slugged down their drinks. No one cheered, but there was respect in many an eye.

"Barkeep," said Remington, "we'll have a word with you."

"I'm busy," said the man.

"Get unbusy right quick then."

"Better do what he says, Lum," said an old-timer at the end of the bar. "And I'll buy all three marshals a drink."

Laughter boiled up out of the crowd and the bartender wiped his hands on his apron, came out from behind to talk to Remington and his partners.

"What you want?" he asked sullenly.

"First of all, there's a man over in the alley behind the saddlery who's shot dead. Name's Willard. Know him?"

"Willard Doolittle. He's the saddler, all right. You kill him?"

"No," said Remington. "A man named Cardiff shot him. The same man who killed those two brothers there, and who shot a U.S. marshal a couple of days ago. You were here then?"

"He was here," said Bucky.

"Yeah."

"You know those boys?" Remington gestured toward the three men sprawled in the sawdust, their blood turning dark in the lantern light.

"I knowed 'em," said Lum.

"What's their connection with Cardiff?"

"You mean the big man? The mean one?"

"That's the one," Remington said dryly.

"The Wymans are trackers, worked with the big man out in the Wyomin' Territory. The other one, Stuckey, he's a bounty hunter or somethin'."

"You mean he's a hired gun," said Bucky.

"Maybe," said Lum. "He come out from Wyomin' Territory about a month or so ago, then he left. And then the three of 'em come in an' they met up with this big feller a few days later. I heard they was lookin' for that nigger Amos and found him, by God." Lum looked at Weede. Jimson's features did not change expression. Nor did he look away or down at his feet. Lum looked away.

"Why'd they come here?" asked Remington.

"Mister, everybody comes here, sooner or later."

"You own this place?"

"I just work here."

"Who owns it?"

"A man named Carberry," said Lum. "Frank Carberry."

Remington looked at Bucky and Jimson.

"So, you knew Amos Washington, too," said Ned. It was not a question.

"Well, he worked for the Carberrys. I never had much use for him myself."

"You said Carberrys. More than one?"

"Frank's got a brother out in Cheyenne. He's some kind of lawman. I ain't seen Owen in six, seven years."

"What did Washington do for the Carberrys?" Remington wanted to know.

"Mister, if I told you what I thought or what I know, I'd be lyin' on the floor like those fellers there by tomorry mornin'. I don't know what he did and I didn't want to know. But Amos, him, and Owen go back a long ways together, before the war."

"I could have you locked up as a material witness," said Remington.

"What's that?" asked Lum.

"Withholding information about a crime is a crime."

"I told you, I don't know nothin'," Lum said stubbornly. "And even if you put me in jail, I wouldn't know nothin'."

"Who would know something?" asked Bucky, his impatience rising like the color that suddenly flushed his cheeks.

"Frank Carberry," said Lum quickly.

"And where would we find him at this time of night?" asked Weede.

"Probably down at the depot. They's a train leavin' at eight o'clock for Kansas City. Frank's goin' there."

"What time is it, now?" Remington wanted to know. The bartender shrugged. One of the men at the bar overheard, pulled a timepiece out of his pocket. It dangled at the end of a woven leather fob.

"Seven of the clock," he said, "give or take five or ten minutes. Or maybe fifteen." He shook the watch, examined it again.

"Bucky, bring up the horses," said Remington. "Jimson, you ask around, see if anyone else knows these boys."

"Yes, sir," said Weede.

Remington turned his attention back to Lum.

"If your name ever comes up again, either here or in Wyoming Territory, Lum, I'll be back and you'll sleep behind bars."

"I ain't broke no law."

"What's your last name?"

"Stout. Lum Stout."

"I'll remember it," said Remington.

"I ain't broke no damned law."

"Better think about it, real fast. I want to know the connection between the Carberrys and Jack Cardiff."

"I don't know. But them other boys worked for Frank and Owen back before the war and Amos worked for them too. I think they was all slavers."

Remington sucked in a breath. Lum spoke so low Ned had barely heard him, but he had understood him. Lum looked around the room to see if anyone had overheard. Slavery was still a touchy issue, even so long after the war. The war itself was a vivid memory in everyone's minds—those who had lived on the bloody Missouri–Arkansas border, especially. There were still bitter feelings among many.

Remington knew about the debates in Washington, District of Columbia, but to the people of Missouri and Arkansas, during those times before the war, the furor had little meaning. The majority of slaveholders lived in the deep South states. His folk and most of the others he knew then had come into the Ozarks from Tennessee and Kentucky, some from Virginia, the Carolinas, and Georgia. Even Ned's parents, who were not slaveholders, were somewhat sympathetic with the South, or at least with those Southerners they knew who treated their slaves well.

Most of the people he had known back then, in the late fifties, early sixties, thought that slavery was not all good, but it wasn't all bad, either. He remembered his father, Amos Langhorne Remington, saying at the time: "Whatever slavery is, it don't mean we got to go to war or secede from the Union. Let them as has slaves keep 'em and treat 'em well and those what don't, mind their own damned business."

Ned learned later on, after he had gone to war, about the passage of the Kansas–Nebraska Bill and about the Kansas–Missouri border warfare. His people had paid it no mind, but he heard talk of the "underground railroad," stories about black slaves leaving the deep South and heading north, following the Big Dipper, calling the constellation the "Drinking Gourd," making up songs they sang in the cotton fields on the big plantations. People sympathetic to these "escapes" set up hiding places for the slaves all through Arkansas and Missouri, using root cellars and spring houses to conceal the runaways. This was a very exciting time for Ned, because, he, like most other people living in Missouri, thought it would all blow over. No one that he knew truly believed that there would be a war, a war that pitted brother against brother, neighbor against neighbor, friend against friend.

Most Missourians tolerated slavery, held that it was neither all good nor all bad. Ned had seen runaway slaves before, seen their hiding places on small farms in northwest Arkansas. He often wondered what happened to them after they went north. Now, it seemed that he had missed something. If the Carberrys were slavers, where did they deal in human flesh, where did they sell the slaves, and to whom?

Weede finished his rounds, walked up to Remington.

"Find out anything?" Ned asked.

"Not much. Most of the men here think those boys were no-accounts."

"Let's go, then."

"Ned, what's Judge Barnstall going to say about all this?" Weede looked at the three dead men.

"He probably won't like it any. I don't like it myself."

The two men left the saloon. The hubbub rose up in their wake. Bucky was waiting outside with the horses. The trio rode off toward the train yards.

* * *

The St. Louis–San Francisco Railway Company had completed laying track to Springfield in 1870, extended the line to Monett that same year. During the war, the train ran only to Sullivan, Missouri, from St. Louis. As the three lawmen rode into the yards, the St. Louis train was sitting at the depot, its boiler chuffing steam and smoke into the night air.

"Keep your eyes open," Ned told his deputies. "I'll see what I can find out."

He climbed down from his horse, hitched it to the rail along one side of the depot. He walked inside. The benches were empty, the clerk's window still open. Remington strode up to it. The clerk appeared a moment later.

"St. Louis?" he said.

"I'm looking for two men," said the marshal. "One is a big feller, the other probably wearing a business suit."

"Nope."

"Nope?"

"I ain't seen either one. Sold tickets to four ladies going in to Chicago to catch the Chicago and Northwestern to Omaha, a pair of beef buyers taking the Kansas Pacific out of St. Louis to Sedalia, and a woman and her daughter going to Dodge on the Atchison, Topeka, and the Santa Fe."

"You're sure?"

"I'm sure, and if you want a ticket to St. Louis, you got ten minutes before that train pulls out."

"Mind if I look around?"

"Look around where? Just who are you, mister?"

"Name's Remington. U.S. Marshal Remington."

"You lookin' for somebody?"

"Those two men. Either one of them."

"Well, I ain't seen anyone in here looks like either one. Every man bought a ticket was short and none was wearing a business suit."

Remington walked outside, looked up at Weede and Kermit who were still sitting on their horses.

"Neither Cardiff nor Carberry has showed up here," said Remington.

"Don't make sense," said Bucky.

"Unless they rode on to Rolla," said Weede.

"They couldn't make it in time," said Ned.

He walked along the train, looked in the windows. A few people looked out at him curiously. He walked down the other side. The clerk had been right. No one matched the description of Cardiff, nor was any man wearing a business suit. He didn't know what Carberry looked like, exactly, but he knew the type.

Ten minutes later, the train pulled out of the yard, its iron wheels gathering momentum, its whistle blowing. The three marshals watched it go. Just before it pulled out of the yard, two riders rode up to the passenger car. One man, a very big man, swung onto the platform. He held out a hand to the other, who was wearing a dark suit, carried a satchel.

"Hold up there!" shouted Remington, putting spurs to his horse.

"That's them!" yelled Bucky.

"Come on, let's get 'em!" Jim Weede galloped ahead of Bucky, slapping his horse's rump with his hat.

The train gathered speed. The two men disappeared inside the car. Gradually, it pulled away, its steam whistle piercing the night.

Remington reined up, waited for Bucky and Jim to catch up.

"Well, I think we got low card in that hand," Ned told them.

"Was that them?" asked Weede.

"It was," said Remington. "That bastard Cardiff grinned at me and waved before he went inside."

"Now what?" asked Bucky.

"We get ourselves some tickets to Cheyenne," said Remington.

"We'll be a day late and a dollar short," said Weede.

"That's what Harry Bellows used to say," said Bucky tonelessly.

"He also said something else," said Remington.

"What's that?" asked Bucky.

"When things went bad for him, Harry always said 'Well, somebody's gonna eat sonofabitch stew and I'm gonna cook it for 'em.'"

The men laughed, but there was an edge of bitterness to their laughter.

The man who had murdered Harry Bellows had gotten away again.

"Let's go get those tickets," said Remington. In the distance, they heard the lonesome wail of the train whistle and the yard turned quiet as a ghost town.

Chapter Five

Remington and his two deputies stepped off the Union Pacific train out of Julesberg, looked at the sign on the depot that said CHEYENNE. It was mid-afternoon and the sky was cloudless, blue as corn-flowers. They carried their duffel to the station platform. Bucky hailed one of the wagons waiting to take passengers into town. The teamster clucked and rattled his reins, drove the rig over to the platform. The marshals loaded their rifles, bedrolls, saddle-bags, clothes into the wagon. Remington sat on the buckboard with the driver.

"We'll need to rent horses," he told the driver, "and see Owen Carberry.

"Took a man there yestiddy," said the driver, a grizzled, wizened man in his late forties. "His brother, I believe."

Remington said nothing.

"You can rent horses at the livery, I reckon. I'll take you there. Gantry's. Bill's a friend of mine. He's honest and keeps good stock."

"You can just point us to Carberry's office from there," suggested Remington.

"Ain't but a block away, next to the Sawtooth Sa-loon and the Laramie Hotel."

"Perfect," said Ned.

On the train out, he had looked through Harry Bellows's daybook more than once. From reading Harry's notes, he gathered that Carberry had not been much help to Harry. There was nothing he could prove, but he had the distinct impression that the town marshal didn't go out of his way to make things easier for the U.S. deputy. At one point, after a fruitless search for a witness, Harry had noted: "Carberry has more excuses than a one-armed juggler."

Another note made more sense since his talk with the bartender in Springfield. Remington thought of it now as the driver urged the team over a rutted road, past weathered shacks that had once housed the track layers. Harry wrote that he had tried to talk to the marshal about Amos Washington, a name that had come up during his investigation. At that time, Washington was still alive, but may or may not have been in Cheyenne. Harry's notes were curt: "Not much information from Carberry. He's a biggeted bastard." Remington chuckled at the spelling of "bigoted," but he vowed to try and probe further into that aspect of Carberry's character.

The driver halted his team in front of Gantry's Livery, set the handbrake.

"Six bits, gennelmen," he said.

Remington paid him in coin. Bucky and Jim threw down the baggage.

"Right over yonder's the marshal's office, twixt the Laramie and the Sawtooth. You don't find Owen in his office, he'll be likely in the saloon. 'Day, gents."

The driver pulled away. Remington walked inside the livery and called out. A man emerged from one of the stalls, carrying a canvas feedbag.

"Yeah? What can I do you for?" he cracked.

"You Bill Gantry?"

"I am. Do I know you?"

"No. I was told you could rent us some horses. I need three, saddles, scabbards, hobbles, martingales."

"Three horses, you say?" Gantry peered through the gloom of the stables, approached cautiously.

"Yes. U.S. Government business."

"Hah. You mean you'll give me a voucher and I'll wait six months to a year for my pay? No, sir. You can try George Abbott over at the stockyards. He might . . ."

"I'm paying cash," said Remington quietly.

"Oh, cash. Well, now, that's different. What's your name, mister?"

Remington told him.

"Well, now, I heard that name somewheres." Gantry came closer and Ned saw that he was a short, stocky man with sloping shoulders, powerful arms. He wore a battered fedora that had once been a nice hat, but was now misshapen, smeared with dirt and horse manure. His face dripped a brushy moustache, and he wore a red bandanna around his neck. A leather vest was open over the light blue chambray shirt he wore, tucked into denims that had patches at the knees. "You a U.S. marshal?"

"I am," said Remington.

"What you lookin' for this time?"

"First time I've been here."

"There was a man named Bellows here before. He had a badge. From someplace in Missoura."

"Galena. Harry was a friend of mine."

"Was?"

"He's dead."

"Sorry. Was he sick?"

"No, he was murdered."

"Sorry, again. That why you're here?"

"Yes," said Remington. "He was killed by a man named Jack Cardiff."

"Christ. Cardiff cuts a wide swath in this town. 'Course, Cheyenne always was a lawless town. Grew too fast, once the U.P. put its tracks down. Brought in a lot of roughs. The damned vigilantes was goin' for a time and there's some as says we still got 'em."

"What do you know about Owen Carberry?"

"Town marshal? Seems to keep the peace. Some say he's in thick with the cattlemen, won't help the sodbusters, but I don't know. Politics. One side tars the other. Both get black. Owen's a hard man, but I can't fault him none."

"He know Cardiff?"

"Well, now, never heard that question asked before. I never seen 'em together. And Cardiff ain't broke no local laws, I know of. Federal, neither."

"I have a warrant for his arrest," said Remington.

"For killing your friend?"

"And for killing Washington. I could swear out a warrant for at least three more murders in Missouri."

"Well, Cardiff's mighty fast with a gun, uses a rifle mostly. He's killed here, too, but it was always ruled self-defense."

"Who made those rulings?" asked Remington.

"Why, Owen Carberry did."

"I'll take those three horses now, Gantry," said Ned.

Owen Carberry looked at the warrant Remington had handed him.

"Appears to be duly signed," he said. He sat behind his desk in the small office on Alder Street. Carberry was a square-jawed, squint-eyed man, lean, his face weathered from sun and wind, his lips cracked, thin, under an aquiline nose. He had pale blue eyes, sandy hair. His badge proclaimed him Town Marshal of Cheyenne, W.T. He wore it on a faded denim jacket. He was shorter than Remington by an inch or two.

"It is," said Remington. "Any idea where I can find Cardiff?"

"He used to sit at the New Idea Saloon, but he left town and I haven't seen him around."

"He's back," said Remington.

"You have proof of that?"

"A pretty good hunch. I think he came here on the U.P. with your brother, Frank."

"Meaning?"

"Meaning I might have to take your brother in for aiding and abetting a fugitive."

"Remington, you better back down." Carberry's eyes narrowed even more, into tight dark slits. "I haven't seen my brother in five or six years."

"I saw him and Cardiff get on the train in Springfield. They were both running. Word I got was that Frank was headed here."

"First I heard of it."

Remington knew that Carberry was lying. The town marshal's eyes were hidden behind those tight slits, but he licked his cracked lips and rattled the warrant in his hand. The two men sat there, sizing each other up as the minutes ticked by.

Remington stood up, pushed the chair to one side. He looked around Carberry's office, at the rifle case, the wanted posters on the walls, the jail keys hanging on a nail, the door to the jail, closed and undoubtedly locked, the bench against the wall, the paperweight made out of a chunk of lead, a quill pen jutting out of an ink bottle.

"You tell your brother I'm looking for him," said Remington.

Carberry thrust the warrant back in the U.S. marshal's hand. Ned took it, folded it up, put it in his shirt pocket. Carberry stood up.

"Look, Remington, I don't like you. I don't like your damned warrant. I could care less about Amos Washington and that deputy marshal the judge sent out here. Washington was in the wrong company. He should have known he couldn't trust a white man, especially a man like Jack Cardiff. And if Cardiff killed Bellows as that warrant says he did, then all I got to say is Bellows was plumb stupid."

"Bellows was a lot of things," said Remington, "but stupid wasn't one of them. Now, I'd like to know what Harry ran into when he came to the territory. He checked in with you, I know."

"He did. He was looking into rustled cattle, but he didn't find out much."

"How did he run into Cardiff?" Remington asked.

"Cardiff and his bunch work for the Cattleman's Association. All pefectly legal. They're a group of ranchers who got tired of having their stock stole, so they formed this outfit. They hired Cardiff as a kind of watchdog."

"A bully, you mean," said Remington.

"Maybe. The settlers are all stirred up. They claim that Cardiff is being used to drive them off their lands, so the cattlemen can move in."

"Any truth to that, Carberry?"

"There might be. Nothing I can prove. I listen to the complaints. From both sides."

"You ever find anything to back up a claim?"

"I've found some altered brands, slaughtered stock. All on settlers' lands."

"Somebody could have stacked the deck."

"Cardiff? It's possible. I'd need proof, though."

"Maybe you don't. If we get Cardiff back to Galena, he'll hang."

"But his bunch won't," snapped Carberry. "There's somebody running Cardiff and I don't know who he is, but he's fifty times the sidewinder Jack is."

"Any idea why your brother would take up with Cardiff?"

Carberry's face flushed crimson.

"I have only your word on that, Remington."

"I'll let it go, for now. But I aim to do some digging and I don't care who it hurts. If something comes up smelling, I'll consider it bad. I'd like to know I could count on your help as a lawman."

"I work my side of the street, Remington. Maybe you ought to think about where you are and why your friend Bellows is dead."

"What do you mean by that, Carberry?"

"All I'm sayin' is that you and your two deputies out there are a long way from home. This is Wyoming Territory and it's got its own laws, its own problems."

"I just hope you aren't one of its problems, Carberry," said Remington.

He touched a pair of fingers to the brim of his hat in salute, then walked out the door. Kermit and Weede were waiting for him.

"I got us one big room, three bunks, at the Laramie," said Bucky. "You do any good in there?"

"Carberry is a bigoted sonofabitch," said Remington, looking at Weede. "He isn't going to be much help, but I need his cooperation. Fact is, he may have helped me more than he wanted to."

"What's our first move?" asked Weede.

"Cardiff frequents a place called the New Idea Saloon. But I think we'll split up. Bucky, you look into things at the New Idea. Jimson, I want you to go to the courthouse and start looking at records—recent land transfers, court cases involving rustled cattle."

"What are you looking for, Ned?" asked Weede.

"I don't know. Something that might pop up, a common thread."

"What about you, Ned?"

"I'm going to look into the Cattleman's Association. It seems to be at the center of all this. Cardiff works for them, and that's the outfit Harry was interested in when he was out here conducting his investigation."

"Where'll we meet?" asked Bucky.

"What room are we in?" Remington grabbed his saddlehorn, pulled himself aboard the rented horse.

"Number twenty. Second floor."

"We'll meet there at six o'clock, hash it all out over supper."

"Fair enough," said Bucky.

"Jim," said Remington, "don't let them give you any trouble at the courthouse."

"You mean because I'm black?"

"That's just what I mean," said Remington grimly.

Remington asked Gantry where he might find the office of the Cheyenne Cattleman's Assocation. The liveryman told him it was on the second story, above Delmonico's Restaurant on Central Avenue. The marshal rode there, passing farmer's carts laden with fresh produce, a passel of boys playing "pie" with

Barlow pocket knives. He saw a few cowboys, several Indians, most Arapaho and Ute, and ladies strolling in and out of the shops along the avenue.

He tied the horse at the hitchrail, looked up at the windows above Delmonico's. There were three, all bearing painted legends: RUPERT P. GOODE, Dentist; ALISTAIR QUINCANNON, Attorney at Law; and THE CHEYENNE CATTLEMAN'S ASSOC. He saw movement in the CA office, noticed the stairs next to the restaurant. The door was unlocked and open.

He climbed the stairs, turned to the right down the hallway. He passed the dentist's office, heard a loud voice coming from the lawyer's place. He opened the door to the Cattleman's Association office and stepped inside.

Something hard jammed into Remington's right side. Cold steel pressed against his neck. He heard the click of a hammer cocking next to his ear.

They had two guns on him. Either one could blow him to hell.

Chapter Six

Remington froze, looked straight ahead through the window he had seen from the street. The letters were backward, but he thought only of the guns, one in his side, the other boring into his neck. The one at his neck was cocked and he was a split-second from eternity.

"Mister, you make one false move and I'll break your neck with a forty-five ball through your spine."

"My name is Ned Remington. I'm a United States marshal."

"Snake his pistol out of that holster, Brad," said the man holding the gun at Remington's neck.

A hand reached out, pulled Remington's pistol from its holster.

"Now, you step out in the middle of the room, mister, and keep looking out that window."

Remington stepped forward. The pressure of the two pistols was no longer on his flesh.

"Turn around. Real slow."

The marshal turned around, looked at the two men behind the door. One wore the town clothes of a rancher, a neat, freshly-ironed shirt, a vest, creased wool trousers, polished boots. He was hatless, hazel-eyed, with sharp, symmetrical features, straight nose, thin lips. He appeared to be in his late thirties, early forties.

The other man wore a cowman's garb, dusty boots, well-worn denims, a faded linsey-woolsey shirt, a hat with a Montana crease. Both wore holster rigs. The cowboy had brown eyes, a nose that looked like it had been made by a mud-dauber, thick lips, ragged teeth. He was the one called Brad, and he had Remington's pistol stuck in his belt.

"Who are you, mister?" asked the rancher.

"I told you."

"He's wearin' a badge, Mr. Packer."

"So, you really are a U.S. marshal?"

"I am," said Remington.

"What do you want?"

"Some information. I have a warrant for the arrest of one Jack Cardiff."

Packer let out a breath, holstered his pistol, a .45 Colt with a four-inch barrel. Lethal at close range. At neck range, Remington thought.

"Give him back his gun, Brad. Mr. Remington, I'm Jesse Packer. I own the Dot J ranch north of Cheyenne. This man's Norman Bradley. He works for me. Come on in the office and I'll buy you a drink."

Brad handed Remington his pistol, smiled sheepishly. The three men shook hands. Packer led the way through another door that lead from the outer office. In contrast to the neatness of the outer office, the inner cubicle was a shambles. Papers lay strewn across the desk and on the floor. Opened boxes littered the open spaces. A plat map on the wall showed the layout of the various ranches, with thumbtacks stuck in various places.

Brad set out a chair for Remington, grabbed one

for himself. Packer sat behind the desk, pushed aside a stack of papers.

"Sorry to have to throw down on you like that, Remington," said Packer, "but you walked smack dab into the middle of a range war. Me and some other ranchers took over the Association's offices yesterday. There was some trouble, and we were expecting some of Delaney's men to come in here today."

"Delaney?"

"Circle D." Packer pointed to the map behind him, touched a brass tack. "John Delaney joined up with Charlie Phipps at the C Bar P and tried to move us off of our water down here, on Lodgepole Creek." The rancher traced a finger along a line on the map.

"They hired Cardiff to move the settlers out," said Brad. "That's when we smelt a skunk."

"We'd have to move up on the Chugwater or the Horse and get into a fight up there with Dave Morriss and some of other ranchers," said Packer. "We go south, to the grasslands, and we run into sheep. So, we've got to protect our lands or Delaney and Phipps will hog it all."

"Does Carberry know about this?" asked Remington.

"He does. It's out of his jurisdiction. But, his brother, Frank, is in with Delaney. Always has been. Fact is, Delaney and Phipps have us outmanned with black men, Negroes."

"Negroes?" Remington felt his flesh crawl. The hackles rose up on the back of his neck.

"Slaves," said Bradley. "We can't prove it, but Amos Washington started to buck Delaney about using the Negroes as fighting men. Cardiff told Washington to keep his mouth shut or he'd kill him.

Washington lit a shuck, but he said he was going to tell everything he knew."

"This goes back a long way," said Packer. "Ten years, maybe."

"What can you tell me about it?" asked Remington.

Packer leaned back in the chair, put his feet up on the desk. Brad moved his chair closer to the window, looked out every once in a while down onto the street. Remington knew they were still expecting trouble.

"Story I heard was that Owen and his brother Frank ran an underground railway before and during the war. Runaway slaves would come up into Arkansas and Missouri, and the Carberrys put them up. But, instead of giving them their freedom, they sold them out here in the territory to ranchers like Delaney and Phipps. They made a deal where they sold the Negroes for a small amount of money and took a share of the profits."

"Can you prove that?" asked Ned.

"No. But, neither Phipps nor Delaney could have made it without that slave labor. There was too much land, not enough money to hire hands. Even after they got over the hump, they kept the black cowboys on. Hell, look at it, Remington. No wages to pay. Washington was the go-between. He was the one who kept the Negroes in line, until Cardiff came in and started rustling and killing black cowboys."

Remington took a deep breath, tried to sort it out in his mind. He still didn't know where Jack Cardiff fit in. He had to know, and now he thought about some of the cryptic notes he had seen in Harry's journal.

"How did Cardiff work? I thought he was hired by the Cattleman's Association to stop the rustling."

Packer laughed. Brad flashed a wry smile. Both men exchanged looks and then Packer's expression hardened.

"You've got it right, up to a point," said the rancher. "There were some killings. Cattle were rustled. Then, this ex—hard-rock miner, Cardiff, comes into town and he makes an offer to clean up the problem. We formed the Cattleman's Assocation. All of us were members at that time. Me, Delaney, Banse, Morriss, Phipps, a couple of others. We voted to hire Cardiff, who had his own men. Hell, it was like buying a fox to guard the chickens."

"But you didn't know that then?" Remington pointed out.

"No. The rustling stopped. There were some dead men brought in by Cardiff. He said they had been caught with running irons. It was all done legal. But, as soon as the rustling stopped, then someone began going after the settlers. Some of us thought it was Cardiff. People started to leave and some of the other ranchers benefited, no doubt about it."

"How did Washington fit in?"

"Some of the Negroes owned by Phipps and Delaney wanted land, and Washington saw to it that they got small homesteads. Then he found out that the blacks didn't actually own the land, nor were they ever likely to. Delaney and Phipps gave their slaves guns and got them to run off settlers. Cardiff was in on that, too."

Remington let out a low whistle of surprise. He began to put together an ugly picture of land-grabbing, greed, murder, and conspiracy. But, it was so complicated, it was no wonder that Harry Bellows had trouble unraveling the scheme. Still, his notes showed that he had been on the right track.

"When did you figure all this out?" asked Remington.

"Just before Amos Washington left the territory, he rode up to my ranch and told me most of it. He said if I would look at the land records, I'd see that what he said was so."

"Did you believe Washington?"

"Not at first. It was a hell of a note. We just didn't want to ride down that road at the time."

"What changed your mind?"

"I looked at the land records. Delaney and Phipps had recorded some new deeds on homesteaded land. Hell, I saw where they would crowd the rest of us right out of the country. The fights in this country have always been over water. I could see a hell of a fight coming."

"Then, what happened?" asked Ned.

"Delaney kept us away from the creek. I had two hands shot. Some others quit. Yesterday, we took over the Association, run Delaney and Phipps out. We expect they'll be back. Or send Cardiff after us. We been lookin' through the records here ever since yesterday."

Remington looked around the room.

"I see," he said. "Find anything?"

Packer rifled through a stack of papers, found what he was looking for and handed several documents to Remington. Ned read them over carefully.

One of the documents was a first draft of a letter requesting that Jack Cardiff be appointed U.S. Marshal of Wyoming Territory, or at least a deputy. Another was a report of a conversation with Harry Bellows dated several months before. Others added to

the picture of an organization attempting to establish
its own authority and law enforcement branch. Taken
together, the documents presented a chilling view of
an organization attempting, in effect, to take the law
into its own hands. The Cattleman's Association,
under Delaney's direction, seemed designed to be-
come a sovereign state within a United States territory.

"Well, Remington, what do you think?" asked
Packer.

"I think we've got a serious problem here."

"Two nights ago, a group of masked riders rode up
to a small rancher's home and shot ten head of cattle
right in front of his door. His cattle. That rancher is
packing up to move out."

"Got a name?" asked Remington.

"Leland Guilder," said Packer. "He and his family
own two thousand acres and Frank Carberry bought
the note from the bank a year ago when Lee was late
with a mortgage payment."

"Any more such evidence?"

"We're digging it out. Not that we know what to
look for, Marshal."

"I'll help you," Ned told him. "I have a man over
at the courthouse now. If we combine our efforts, I
think I can bring a case against Delaney, Phipps, Carberry, and the others."

"Be too damned late," said Brad. "Delaney's gone
hog wild. There's a homesteader who filed on a section of land, him and his family, on both sides of
Lodgepole. It's land that Delaney wants bad."

Remington was seized with the enormity of the
problem. He had stepped into the middle of a range
war that was gathering momentum even as they sat
there. Delaney and his bunch were apparently well

organized. They had been in operation for a long time. Greed. It stuck out in every document he had read, in every aspect of what he had heard. Greed and the lust for power.

"What did you plan to do?" asked Remington. "Were you going to help the homesteader?"

"Jensen? Hell, he hates cattlemen with a passion. But, we had thought about it. If Cardiff and his bunch goes in there, Jensen won't have a chance. There'll be blood spilled."

"Well, maybe that's our first priority."

"How many men did you bring with you?" asked Bradley.

"There are three of us," said Remington softly.

A silence filled the room. Brad smiled wryly, but at least he didn't laugh out loud. Remington gave him that. Still, he had the feeling that Packer couldn't bring many men into a full-fledged fight.

"We're mighty short-handed," said Brad, as if reading the marshal's thoughts.

"We're looking for Cardiff now," said Remington. "I have a man over at the New Idea right now, trying to pick up his trail."

"Haw," laughed Brad. "He'll be about as welcome as a heathen at a prayer meetin'."

"Bucky can handle himself," said Remington.

"Reason Cardiff goes there is because he feels right at home," said Brad. "Every hardcase in the territory hangs around the New Idea. If you wanted to get an army up, that's where you'd go to find ready guns."

"Might be something to keep in mind," said Remington cryptically. Packer smiled knowingly.

"Uh oh," said Brad, peering out the window. "Here comes trouble."

Packer got up, went to the window. Remington came up behind the two men, looked down. Three riders came up the street. One of them looked familiar.

"That's Delaney himself," said Packer.

"And his segundo, Morty Rittenhouse," said Brad.

"The other man is Frank Carberry, if I'm not mistaken," said Remington.

"By God, you're right," said Packer. "He ain't changed much. The sonofabitch."

The three men looked up at the window, turned their horses toward the hitchrail.

"He's coming to take back what we took from him," said Brad, who always seemed to bore right in on the point of a thing.

"Marshal, there may be a fight yet today," said Packer.

Remington stepped back from the window. He looked at Packer.

"Just how much right does he have to come up here?" asked the marshal.

"Not as much as I have," replied Packer. "He took over the organization, but there was no legal meeting, no quorum. He just took it over."

"So, who was president before that?"

"I was," said Packer. "And, by God, I still am."

"That's good enough for me," said Remington.

Packer was a man such as the marshal was used to dealing with. He seemed to be a man of his word. That was more than he could say for some, but in the West, a man's word was often all he had as collateral. If you could not believe a man, he was not to be trusted. If you trusted a man, his word was all you needed to seal any bargain, make good on any note.

Packer was just such a man, Remington was convinced.

It seemed to him that Delaney and his bunch didn't have a leg to stand on. They ignored the rules and laws of a duly constituted body, and took what they wanted without regard to due process. Remington had learned much of the law from Judge Barnstall. As chief deputy U.S. marshal, he was expected to know and follow the law. He was also expected to uphold it whenever he encountered a serious threat to its foundations. Now he found himself in just such a position. Although he had made a snap judgment in Packer's case, he was certain that he was doing the right thing.

He knew enough about the Cheyenne Cattleman's Association to know that it was a legal organization, incorporated in the territory of Wyoming. Therefore, only an election by its members or a legal board decision could remove its president from office. If Packer said he was still in charge, Remington believed him.

Bradley leaned out the window, looked down below.

"They're tyin' up their horses," he said.

"Are they wearing guns?" asked Packer.

"Can't tell. I don't see no rifles."

"Marshal, any suggestions?" asked Packer.

"I'd just play the hand as it's dealt. Expect trouble, but don't look for it."

"Right."

"I wouldn't jump them, like you did me," advised Ned. "Why don't you and Bradley wait here. I'll go in the outer office and see what they want."

"Good idea," said Packer.

"We'll be ready if there's any trouble," said Bradley.

Remington went into the outer office, stood off in a corner by the window. He looked out at the street below, waited for the sound of footsteps down the hall. It was quiet. The seconds dragged into minutes. Remington again looked out the window. He heard a horse nicker, saw the swick of a tail, the rump of a horse. He could not see the riders who had hitched up to the rail.

A sound down the hall jangled his senses. He tensed, listening for the hollow sound of bootheels on the hardwood flooring. Instead, he heard only the faint creak of a board, a sound like water sloshing in a pail.

Remington moved toward the door. Something was wrong. He sensed it, but could not put a name to the fear that began to gnaw at his senses, tighten his gut. A board creaked again, as if someone was walking barefoot down the hall. He heard more splashing sounds, and a warning bell sounded in his brain.

He started to open the door, heard the muffled sound of low voices at the end of the hall.

Perhaps, he thought, someone had come up to see the dentist, or the lawyer. Ned put his ear to the door, floated his right hand to the butt of his pistol.

He heard, then, a sound like the crackling of leaves in autumn when the breeze is up, or a deer stalks through the woods. Crackle, crackle. Then, he heard a sound like a sudden wind springing up, and a whoosh, like winter air coming down a chimney.

He stepped back away from the door, his senses flaring at full alert. He reached for the door handle.

That's when he heard the terrible scream.

Remington's blood froze as his hand touched the handle of the door.

Again the scream, piercing, shrill, hurtling down the hall, tearing at his eardrums.

It was a woman's scream and it came from down the hall.

Remington lifted the handle, jerked open the door.

A hail of gunfire broke out, popping in the stillness, and underneath it, the roar, the horrible roar, like a great wind surging through a mountain pass.

Remington knew, then, what it was. He had heard such a sound before.

And the screaming rose in pitch until it blotted out all sound, knotted all thought.

A rush of hot air drove Remington back into the room, and smoke assailed his nostrils.

"Fire!" Someone yelled from down the hall.

Then Remington smelled the burning coal oil and knew that they were trapped in a fiery furnace of hell.

Chapter Seven

Smoke boiled into the room, and the bristling sound of flames crackled under the noise of gunfire. Glass shattered as bullets sprayed through the window. Remington heard Brad yell, and moments later the next room boomed with the sound of return fire.

"Packer, Bradley, get out!" Remington yelled.

He ducked down, opened the door to the other office as bullets ricocheted around the front room. The woman's screams stopped, but the hallway roared with the sound of flames sweeping through it like fire in a blast furnace.

The rancher and his foreman lay on the floor. The walls were riddled and pocked with bullet holes. Glass shards lay strewn on the desk and on some of the tables.

"The building's on fire," said Remington. "We have to get out, now!"

"What about these records?" asked Packer, lifting his head.

"Take what you can," said Remington. "Then, throw the rest out the window. We have to move quick."

"We'll have to shoot our way out," said Bradley.

As if to emphasize his words, another rifle shot

cracked from outside and a bullet whined through the vacant window. Remington hugged the doorway.

"Come on," he said. "Move!"

Packer and Bradley scrambled to their feet. Packer grabbed a sheaf of papers, stuffed them inside his shirt. Bradley did the same. They began throwing cartons out the window. The cartons rolled down the roof, fell to the street below. Horses whinneyed. More rifle shots boomed, and the two men windmilled away from the shattered window. Remington grabbed Bradley's arm, pulled him into the outer office.

"Come on, Packer," he shouted, racing to the hall door.

Remington peered out. He saw the wall of flames at the other end of the hall, saw tongues of fire eating at the wallpaper, licking at the baseboards. There was no way out that way. At the far end of the hall, he saw another door, past the second Cattleman's Association office. Perhaps, he reasoned, there were outside stairs leading downward. Quickly, he ran to the door. He jerked it open. There was an outside stairway.

"This way," he said.

With a roar, the flames in the hallway burst toward them, following a path of coal oil. Remington saw Packer come into the hall, carrying a box of papers.

"Hurry!" Remington said. In a moment, he knew, they would be engulfed in flames.

Packer lurched toward him as a wall of flame rose up from the floor and lashed out at him. He leaped forward. Remington drew his pistol and stepped onto the landing. He saw a man in the street below, leveling a rifle at him. He hammered back as he brought his .44 to bear. He squeezed off a shot, saw the man stagger and go down. He started down the stairs.

Bradley came out of the building a second later, followed by Packer. Choking on smoke, Packer stumbled, crashed into Bradley. Fueled by the air let in from the open doorway, the flames in the hallway exploded into the association's offices. The entire top story of the building was now in flames.

Remington took the stairs two at a time, holding his pistol at the ready.

People began shouting, running out of the restaurant below. Remington heard women scream. He hit the bottom of the stairs, dashed into the street, hunched into a fighting crouch.

He heard the thunder of horses' hooves, saw men riding away. Smoke billowed out over the street. He heard, somewhere far off, the clang of a bell. The man he had shot lay sprawled in the street, his rifle still gripped in his hands.

Packer and Bradley half fell, half staggered down the stairs, joined Remington in the street. Papers lay strewn everywhere, and people stared at them, ran from the heat of the burning building. Moments later, a team of horses pulling a fire wagon rounded the corner at full speed. The wagon teetered on two wheels, righted itself. A bucket brigade began to form as people ran up, carrying pails of water.

"Let's go after 'em!" shouted Packer.

"Stay where you are," said Remington. "Start gathering all those papers."

Bradley started to protest, but Remington dashed toward the stairway leading up to the second floor of the building.

"Hey, Remington, where you goin'?" he yelled.

Ned disappeared through the doorway. He climbed

the stairs, halted at the landing. The hallway was a roaring inferno. He hunkered low, looked down the corridor. He saw the woman sprawled in the doorway of the first office. She appeared to be unconscious.

Beyond her, the hall pulsed with flame and smoke. The open doorway at the end sucked the air through it, drawing the flames toward the end of the building. Ned crawled like a lizard toward the lifeless form of the woman. The heat was intense, but most of the wood in that end of the hallway had burned away, leaving gaping holes in the walls. He choked on the smoke, gasped for breath.

There was a layer of air just above the flooring. Four inches, Remington figured. Enough to breathe, if he was careful. He inched his way forward, pausing to wipe gobs of sweat from his sodden brows. He crawled closer to the woman, saw that she had blond hair. It draped her shoulders, fell midway to her waist. He reached out, touched her arm.

He pulled her from the doorway. He heard her moan as he lifted her head slightly. She was still alive, still breathing.

Her eyelids quivered, her lashes fluttered. Remington pulled her into the hallway, started scooting backwards, pulling her with him. Suddenly, he felt the flooring begin to give way. The boards sagged as the voracious fire ate at the beams underneath. In a few moments, he knew, the whole floor would begin to collapse as the flames found fresh fodder underneath. He could already see places where the fire had found new paths to travel, breaches that widened with every passing moment.

He heard a beam crack and seconds later a section of hall fell downward, sending an eruption of sparks upward through the gaping hole. The woman stirred, moaned again. The flooring began to sag and Remington knew if he didn't move fast they might both slide down into the hole several yards away. They would never get out alive if that happened, he knew.

Ned stood up on shaky legs, put his arms under the woman's armpits. He pulled her upward, threw her over one shoulder. She was light. He turned, braced himself, and headed for the stairs. The flames roared louder now, and chunks of ceiling began to break loose, fall to the hall flooring. The open offices roared like blast furnaces as flames devoured papers and wood, melted nails and clay pottery, glass, and china.

Remington's clothing began to smoke as the heat sucked out the moist sweat soaking the fibers. He felt the heat on his flesh as he staggered toward the landing. The floor swayed under his feet, became more unstable as crossbeams and braces burned away. He knew there were only seconds left before the whole floor collapsed.

Flakes of ashes flew through the hallway. The firelight daubed streaks of orange across Remington's face, only to rearrange the patterns again and again. His face glistened with sweat that dried and steamed, then was replenished from overworked glands that struggled to cool his flesh in the searing heat.

The wall to the left of the stairwell sagged, then bulged. Remington reached the landing, took a tentative step down the stairs. He watched the bulging wall with wide-eyed wariness. He paused. Then, as he knew it would, the wall burst and huge tongues of flame burst through the fissure. He felt the stairs sway and knew they would go down. He stepped backward, back onto the landing, and the landing lurched sickeningly, began to teeter as the office wall collapsed under a wall of flame.

The stairs shuddered then, and he felt the bottom go out from under his feet. He plunged downward, clutching the girl's legs tightly to keep her from flying away from him. Downward, downward, he fell and above him, sparks flew like arrows from hell. He braced himself for the landing that never seemed to come, and as he fell, he saw the flames plunge downward as the office flooring gave way Chairs, desks, furniture, all aflame, crashed downward into the murky blackness of the restaurant. A sound, like a gigantic explosion, blotted out the crackle and roar of flames as the building caved in from the top, hurling thunderbolts of fire into the dark pit.

Jim Weede heard the clang of the firebell, dropped the large book on the counter, and raced to the window. He saw people streaming down the street, running as fast as they could, and then he saw the billowing smoke rising over the false-fronted buildings, gathering like angry clouds above a section of the city.

"Fire!" someone yelled.

Weede dashed out of the room and headed for the street. People burst out of offices and galloped for the doorway. The black marshal melded into the running throng, found himself running toward the center of excitement. He saw Buckey Kermit a few moments later, heading in the same direction.

"What's going on?" he yelled.

"I don't know," called back Bucky, "big fire."

"I heard shots a while ago. Sounded like firecrackers."

"Let's go," said Bucky, pumping his stubby legs to keep up with Weede.

The two marshals rounded the corner, saw the bucket brigade falling back from the burning building, the heat so intense they shielded their faces with their arms. They saw a pair of men talking with Owen Carberry in the middle of the street.

"Anybody inside?" asked Weede, as he came up to the town marshal.

"Remington's in there," said Carberry.

Packer and Bradley introduced themselves, told Bucky and Jim what had happened.

"We got out, then he went back inside."

"Why?" asked Kermit.

"I don't know," said Packer. "But that building's going to burn to the ground."

"Shit," said Bucky, ducking behind his arm as waves of heat and ash blew toward them.

Seconds later, they heard a crash, saw the roof collapse over the dentist's office. Flames spewed up into the sky. Black and white smoke belched out of the restaurant. Windows blew outward, and the cluster of men had to retreat to shelter. The air filled with needles of glass and splinters of wood as the heat inside the building intensified.

"No one could get out of there alive," said Carberry.

"I think Frank set that fire," said Packer.

"Watch yourself, Packer. I might get to thinking you had something to do with it."

Kermit and Weede exchanged glances. They stood across the street, watching the coiling, twisting flames, the billows of smoke. The fire raced across the remainder of the roof and the collapse continued to the lawyer's office.

"Look!" shouted Bradley. "Somebody's in Delmonico's. They're tryin' to get out!"

"They're trapped!" yelled Packer.

Weede looked, saw the figure of a man carrying something over his shoulder. It was just a shadow behind the flames, but the man was heading toward the end of the building, beneath the Cattleman's Association offices.

"It's Ned," he said softly. "Bucky, we've got to try and help him."

"Come on," said Bucky. He ran across the street, Weede following. The heat pounded at him, scorched his face and hands. Another section of roof collapsed, and the figure inside the restaurant disappeared as flames jetted into the unfired section.

"He won't make it," said Weede.

Flames drove the two deputies back. They huddled there, helpless, as beams collapsed, walls caved in, and windows blew outward, sending lethal shards of glass flying in all directions.

"Jesus," muttered Bucky.

Remington felt the force of the flame-generated winds inside the restaurant. An exploding beam drove him to his knees. He lurched upright, staggered toward the dark end of the restaurant. The woman on his shoulder struggled, sobbed in his ear. He could not carry her much longer.

He crashed into a table, went down again. He got up, shifted the woman's weight on his shoulder, headed toward the last window at the end of the room. The pane shivered under the building pressure of heat and fiery air.

Remington knew he could wait no longer. He and the woman were in danger of suffocation, now. The flames leeched all of the oxygen out of the room, gobbled it voraciously. He saw tongues of fire darting from cracks in the ceiling. Behind him, the wall of fire moved relentlessly, pressing forward, lapping at his heels like dogs from hell.

He summoned the last of his remaining strength and broke into a ragged lope, heading toward the window. The burning building groaned. Chunks of board and beam fell to the floor in a fiery display that released thousands of winking fireflies into the churning air. Ned turned his back on the window and hurled himself through it. The glass shattered and a rush of hot air drove him into the outside air with the force of a hurricane. He fell on his rump, pulled the woman off his shoulder and into his arms.

He cradled her, forced himself to get to his feet as the hot winds blew at his face. He wrenched himself away from the building and out into the street. Behind him, the rest of the roof collapsed and a huge ball of flame belched through the vacant windows.

Bucky and Jimson rushed up to him, grabbed him by the shoulders, pulled him away from the cloud of fire that clawed at the shirt on his back. He held the woman close to him and ran on wobbly legs. His trousers were so hot now they scorched his flesh and his shirt felt as if someone was running a hot iron over it, pressing it to his raw skin.

Blinded by his own sweat, he felt the last of his strength ebb as the buildings on the opposite side of the street loomed closer. The feeling went out of his legs. They turned to rubber and gave way under him. He went down, and the blackness enveloped him. He heard muffled shouts, as if people were talking underwater or through wads of cotton stuffed in their mouths.

He tumbled into oblivion, into the darkness where it was cool and there was no pain.

Chapter Eight

Her face floated in the mist, framed by delicate blond hair. A pair of blue eyes looked at him, blue like opals, and he thought she was smiling. She was very young, and she was beautiful, with an upturned nose, a dazzling smile. Her teeth were even and bright, white as snow, and he felt the warmth of her, a cool warmth, like summer rain.

"Mr. Remington," she said. "Can you hear me? Are you awake?"

His head was full of thunder, ached with the stone bruises of an intense pain. Memory came and went like shroud-wisps of smoke. He tried to focus on the woman's face, but it blurred and twisted. A strange buzzing sounded in his ears.

"A drink," he said. His lips felt thick, dry. "Water."

"Yes, of course," she said, and her voice sounded far away.

Remington sat up in the soft bed. He heard voices from the other room, footsteps. His nostrils still stung with the acrid aroma of smoke. Memory flooded back in on him and now he remembered the girl he had carried from the burning building. When? He looked around the room. The furnishings were simple: a bureau with a porcelain pitcher and bowl, a small mirror, a table, two chairs, curtains on the windows, Currier & Ives prints on the knotty-pine walls, a nightstand, and the bed on which he lay—iron, functional, complete with creaking bed slats and a mattress full of feather ticking. Yet the sheets were clean and fresh. It was a room such as might be found in a boarding house or a modest hotel. Where was he? Was the woman he had seen the same one as he had rescued?

She came in a few moments later, bearing a tray. On the tray were a clear glass jar of water, a glass, a bottle of brandy.

"I'm Amy Blackmer," she said. "You saved my life. I'll be forever grateful."

She sat on the edge of the bed, poured the glass full of water. She handed it to him.

"How long have I been here?" he asked, surprised at the hoarseness of his voice. It felt like his throat was full of sand. The curtains were drawn and he could not see out the window. Yet there was light, light enough to see, light enough so that no lamp was lit.

"A few hours. Your friends brought you here. This is my home, such as it is. This was my brother's room."

Remington drank greedily. The cool water soothed his parched throat. He finished one glass and she poured another. He drank that down, too.

He coughed.

"You swallowed a lot of smoke," she said.

"My throat is sore."

"No wonder. Mr. Remington, I can't thank you enough for getting me out of that building. I wouldn't be here if it wasn't for you. Do you want some brandy?"

He shook his head. "What were you doing there?"

"I'm a bookkeeper. The dentist's office was closed. I was doing his books when I heard noises. I smelled smoke and when I tried to leave . . ."

"Was there anyone else in there?"

She bowed her head, looked at her hands folded in her lap.

"An attorney and his client. They died in the fire."

"Did you see who set the fire?"

"No," she replied.

He scanned her face, saw that she was telling the truth. She looked remarkably fresh after her ordeal, with her hair combed back away from her face, a touch of rouge on her cheeks. She was very beautiful, young, with a strong chin, comely cheekbones. He liked her.

"Your friends are in the other room," she said. "They want to talk to you. Marshal Carberry wants you to come by his office when you can. He has some questions he wants to ask you."

Remington didn't say what was on his mind regarding Carberry. Instead, he nodded. He drank a half a glass of water, set the empty glass back on the tray.

"Much obliged for tending to me," he said. "I don't remember much about it. Everything went black."

"The doctor said it was the smoke. He said you could have died in there. Both of us could have died."

She arose from the bed. Remington swung his legs over the side.

"Your boots are on the other side," she said.

"How do you feel?" he asked.

"Shaky inside. I didn't inhale much smoke, apparently. I feel like I've had a sunburn. The doctor, Dr. Rumley, said that being unconscious and lying on the floor probably was the best thing that could have happened to me. I don't remember much about it. I know I tripped over a chair or a bench and fell. I think I hit my head on the door when I fell. There was so much smoke. I held my breath, but I couldn't see. I was terribly frightened, too."

"I don't blame you," he said. "But you don't look like a woman who's easily frightened."

Her eyes flashed.

"I'm afraid of fire," she said simply, and he knew what she meant.

"Where is your brother?" he asked. The room was neutral. It didn't look like anybody had ever lived there for very long.

"He's—he died a few months ago. He—he was shot."

"I'm sorry," said Remington. "What happened?"

"Rustlers," she said bitterly. "Dave rode for the B Bar B ranch."

"I don't know the brand."

"Faron Banse. He's just a small rancher. Dave was shot in the back. I—I gave all his things away. I just couldn't bear looking at his room, knowing he would never come back."

"I understand," said Ned.

"Well," she sighed, "enough of that. Your friends are anxious to see you."

She turned, then, and left the room. Remington followed her into the hallway.

"Follow me," she said.

Kermit and Weede got up from their chairs when Amy and Remington entered the room.

"Howdy, Ned," said Bucky. "You have a good nap?"

"Bucky, Jim. I slept some, I reckon."

Weede grinned wide. Kermit's smile was less toothy. They both slapped Remington on the back. Amy stood by, watching the three men.

"Makes yourselves at home," she said. She set down the tray. "There's some brandy here, if you like."

"No, we've got to be going," said Remington. "I thank you again, Miss Blackmer."

"Please, call me Amy. Are you sure you're ready to . . ."

"We have some things needing doing," said the chief marshal. "I'll be seeing you, ma'am."

"Yes, you are welcome here. You and your deputies, Marshal."

She opened the door for them. Remington stepped out onto the porch, looked around the quiet neighborhood. Amy's small frame house was on a wide street, with other houses nearby, but none crowding hers. She had a small front yard, fenced in. The porch was roofed by a portico. Flowers grew along the clapboard fence. Three horses, the ones they had rented, stood hitched to the top board.

Remington waved goodbye to Amy as Kermit closed the gate. The three men mounted. Weede let out.

"How long was I in there?" Remington asked.

"About four hours," said Bucky. "You looked plumb green around the gills when we brung you here. Woman insisted on it."

"I still feel full of smoke," Remington rasped.

"You ate a couple of bushels," said Weede.

"Where we goin'?" asked Remington, reining up

as the Blackmer house disappeared from view. He looked at the sky. The sun was almost down. It hung in the sky until almost nine in the evening at that time of year, midsummer. So, he had been unconscious for a spell.

"Owen Carberry's, I reckon," said Bucky. "He said to bring you by when you came to."

Remington shook his head.

"No, we'll not dance to Carberry's tune," Ned told them. "I don't know how much you boys saw, but I'll tell you what happened as I know it."

"We've been hoping you would," said Jimson. "We got to the fire just about the time you got out and we couldn't make sense of the jabber."

"Did you talk to any witnesses?" asked Ned.

"As many as we could," said Weede. "Nobody really saw anything. Nobody told us who set the fire."

"Do you know, Ned?" asked Bucky.

Ned told them about Packer and Bradley. "We met them," said Bucky. He told them about Frank Carberry and two other men riding up to the restaurant, about hearing footsteps on the stairs, the splash of coal oil, the fire itself. He told it quick and neat.

"Packer said he and Brad would be at the ranch," said Bucky. "They got most of the papers loaded in a wagon. Marshal Carberry wanted to confis—con-scus—he wanted to put them papers in custody, but Packer wouldn't let him."

"Good for him," said Remington. "Let's get to the hotel and plan our investigation from here on. Jim, did you do any good at the courthouse?"

"I think so. Lot a land transfers in the past year or so. Last six months, even more. I took notes." The black deputy patted his saddlebag to show Remington where he had the papers stored.

"How about you, Bucky? Did you pick up any tracks on Cardiff?"

"Jack Cardiff is a kind of local hero," said Kermit. "At least in the New Idea. You mention his name there and you'd better say it friendly-like. But, I heard some talk that the CA was out of business and Cardiff was still working for that Delaney you mentioned."

"That fits," said Remington. "Anything else?"

"People in Cheyenne think the strongest man's gonna win this range war and be top dog. They see Cardiff as being in line as one of the rich men to come out on top."

"Cardiff's name on any of those deeds?" Remington asked Weede.

"Didn't see it."

"All right, let's ride by the burned-out building before we go to the hotel," said Remington. "I want to have a look around."

The building had burned to the ground. The bucket brigades and the firemen were still watering down the neighboring structures. There were hot spots among the rubble, plumes and tendrils of smoke still testifying to the intensity of the blaze. Men pumped the water troughs full and others carried pails of water to the ashes and doused them. Steam hissed, ashes fluttered into the air.

"Wait here," said Remington, dismounting. He handed the reins to Weede, walked toward the left end of the building, where the fire had started. He kicked aside partially burned boards, poked through debris until he found what he sought. He reached down, found the handle, pulled the can out of the pile of ashes. A few feet away, he found another square can, like the first one. He sniffed both of them, carried them out to the street.

"Coal oil," he told his deputies.

"I believe you," said Bucky.

"Bought in some shebang close by, likely," said Weede.

"No," said Remington, "we won't do anything but waste time by asking. I figure these to be from the restaurant, maybe cooking oil. Somebody emptied them, put coal oil in them. Hid them until today."

"You put a lot together with two old burned cans," said Weede, a trace of respect in his tone.

"Cans like these would clatter and ride hard on a saddle," said Ned. "When those three men rode up, they weren't carrying tin luggage."

"All right," said Weede. "What now?"

Remington set down the cans, kicked each one back across the street. Men stared at him with empty eyes, blank expressions. The cans rattled across the street, end over end until they stopped.

"Let's go to the hotel and make map," said Remington, iron in his voice. He took the reins from Weede, hauled himself into the saddle. His jawline tautened. A muscle quivered in his cheek. Bucky and Jimson exchanged looks, but never said a word.

The sun fell over the horizon as the three men rode up to the Laramie Hotel, tied their mounts to the hitchrail. The street began to fill with shadows, and lamps flickered on in the saloons, spilling pale light on the boardwalks.

Bucky got the key to their room from the desk clerk. The lobby was empty at that time of the evening. The three men strode upstairs. The hallway was dark, but a man struck a match, lit a taper. He held it to a lamp attached to the wall. For a moment, his face was bathed in soft flame. Remington looked at him briefly. There was something familiar about the man, but the match went out before the taper was lit. The man coughed loudly as the three men passed him by. He did not strike another match right away, but stood there as Bucky, followed by Remington and Weede, stopped in front of the door to their room.

"Uh oh," he said. He didn't use the key, but pushed against the door. It swung open, silent on oiled hinges. The room held the last of the light, teemed with shadows. The three marshals drew their pistols, stepped inside.

The man down the hall coughed again. Weede, annoyed, started to go back into the hall. Remington stopped him, put a finger to his lips. Bucky went into a crouch. Something scraped against a table in the far corner of the large room.

Remington heard a soft click, as a sear engaged on the hammer and trigger mechanism of a pistol.

"Watch out!" he whispered.

Orange flame exploded into a flowering blossom that made the darkness crackle with light. Three quick shots sounded as the marshals dove for the floor. Blinded, they rubbed their eyes. They heard noises, the rattle of a window pane. Remington saw a dark shape fill the pale opening. He brought his pistol up, hammered back. Then, as he squeezed the trigger, the shape disappeared, outside, onto the portico roof attached to the false front. Glass shattered as his bullet smashed out the pane.

"Too high!" he cursed.

They heard footsteps on the roof, footsteps pounding down the hall, away from them.

"Jimson. Get the man in the hall," yelled Remington, scrambling to his feet. "Bucky, come on."

Remington dashed to the window. He smashed into a table, kicked it aside. His boots crunched glass underfoot as he climbed through the open window. He crawled out onto the roof, saw a man swing over the side, drop to the street below. The marshal felt his boots slide on the slick shingles. He leaned away from the pull of gravity, approached the roof edge cautiously. He heard nothing as he peered over the eave, looked down at the street. Whoever had jumped off, had slipped alongside the building, perhaps to the alley behind.

Remington paused, listened. He heard nothing for several seconds. Then, he heard horses gallop away down the alley. Two of them, he figured. Two men. Now he recalled the man in the hallway, knew why he had seemed familiar. He had seen that face before. Jesse Packer, or Bradley, had pointed the man out earlier that day. He was Delaney's segundo—what was his name? Ritter? No, Rittenhouse. Morty Rittenhouse. Who, then, was the man in the room?

Remington cursed himself for being stupid. He turned back toward the window.

"See 'em?" asked Bucky.

"No, they got away. I know one of them. The other might be John Delaney. Or Frank Carberry."

Remington sidled back across the roof, climbed through the window. Bucky struck a match, lit one of the lamps. Moments later, Jim Weede returned, shaking his head, panting for breath.

"He got away," he said. "He went around back and jumped on a horse."

"You see the other man?" asked Remington.

Weede shook his head. "Too dark," he wheezed.

Remington looked around the room. It was a shambles. Their bedrolls were tossed against the wall, the bunks lay in disarray. Personal items lay strewn in all directions.

"Somebody was sure lookin' hard for something," observed Kermit.

"Yeah," said Weede.

Remington said nothing. He looked through his saddlebags, picked up his bedding, tossed it on a bunk. He opened one of the saddlebags, took out a cloth sack of hardtack, jerky, a pair of airtights, a can of beans, a can of peaches. Finally, he pulled out an object wrapped tightly in oilcloth. He unwrapped it slowly.

"Close and lock the door, Bucky," he said.

Bucky closed the door, latched it tight, bolted it.

Remington held up the book, showed it to the two deputies.

"What is it?" asked Weede.

Bucky answered him. "Looks like that book Harry always was writin' in."

"It is," said Ned. "Harry's daybook, his diary. That's probably what those jaspers were looking for."

"What's it got in it?" asked Weede.

"Maybe some of the answers we're looking for," said Remington. "Maybe some clues that will save us a lot of time."

"Who would know you'd have that book?" asked Bucky.

Remington smiled wryly.

"Someone who knew Harry before, who saw him with the book. Someone who might figure I'd get hold of it."

"Like who?" asked Weede.

"Like somebody who'd kill to take it away from me."

The two deputies looked at Remington for a long moment, but he said no more. Instead, he opened the book, began leafing through its pages.

Somewhere, he thought, Harry Bellows had written something down that had seemed important at the time. And, someone had known that he might have written it down, or maybe had seen him do it.

There were names in the daybook. Names aplenty. Some of them he had heard this very day, and some he could now put faces to.

It was a hell of a game they were playing. Harry had guessed that it was bigger than anyone else imagined. He had paid dearly for not finding out sooner just how big the stakes were.

Remington let out a breath, looked at his two companions.

"I'm tired of being shot at, burned up, and ransacked," he said. "Now, we go hunting."

Bucky and Jimson smiled.

"About goddamned time," said Weede, grinning wide.

Chapter Nine

The three marshals sat at the table in their room long and late that night, candlewax dripping into a dish as they scribbled notes, poured over Harry's daybook, and drew crude maps, laying out all the important ranches around Cheyenne. Their quarters looked like a war room, with plates of halfeaten food stacked on the bureau, a bottle of whiskey nearly emptied, coffee cups on the windowsills.

Flickering lamps etched their faces in light and shadow. A light breeze blew at the curtains framing the open windows. It was hot in the room. Weede sat shirtless, his chair turned backwards. Bucky wore only shorts and an undershirt, his pistol dripping from the back of his chair, in handy reach. Remington had the front of his shirt unbuttoned, his boots off, leaned over the table, hatless, scrawling a route they might take on the morrow.

"We'll press them hard," said Remington. "We'll ride together and we'll make them sweat."

"Where to first?" asked Bucky.

"Start at the top, work our way down."

"Delaney?"

"That's right," replied Ned. "Then Phipps,

Morriss . . . who else do you have on your list, Jimson?"

"Banse, Packer . . ."

"Good enough. We'll see Packer, too. Meanwhile, how long will it take you, Jim, to make sense out of the notes you took at the courthouse?"

"Day or so, I reckon."

"Bring your notes," said Remington. "Bucky, we're going to make a wide loop and shorten it up. I want Cardiff. And I want to bring Frank Carberry in close, too. I want to talk to him, man to man."

"What about Owen Carberry?"

"If I turn over even one bad stone and find any trace of Owen Carberry under it, I'll put him in irons," said Ned.

"Good!" chorused the two deputies.

"Now, let's get some shut-eye. We'll get started early, before daylight."

"I'd like to look over these notes first," said Weede. "I just wrote down a lot of transfers and coded them for the sake of speed. I still have to sort them out."

"Do what you have to do," Remington told him. "Anything you want to talk about now?"

Weede looked long and hard at Remington, then shook his head.

"Not just yet," said the black man. "It's a jumble."

"All right. Bucky?"

"I'll be thinking of everything I heard in the New Idea today," he said. "But I'm hitting my bunk. I'm plumb wore down to a nub."

Remington laughed. He got up, turned down one of the lamps. Bucky fell on his bunk, Weede moved over to the table. Ned walked to a window, lifted the shade. He looked down at the empty street, the flickering lamp at the corner. Cheyenne had grown up some, it seems, from a railroad town to a cattle town. Like many such, it had not grown well.

Ten or eleven years ago, he knew, there wasn't even a town here. He, like many others, had heard the story of how the city came to be. Once, Ned had run into a photographer who had worked with the surveying parties when the Kansas Pacific was looking for a route back in the sixties. Bill Bell had a keen eye and a good ear. He did a lot of looking, and he told Ned how the railroad men were building the West.

"They lay the rails," he said, "further and further away from the East. There's lots of land out there in the West, and as the rails get closer to all that land, the price of land, lots in a town, say, keeps getting higher and higher. Money. Boil all the vegetables away and that's what it gets down to—money. The surveyors point the way and the rails come in. They build a terminal depot. Business. That's where it starts and they start going for the Western trade. They ship the goods, and the goods are needed out there on the prairie, in the mountians, and beyond, and they send them to Denver, to Santa Fe, to Fort Union, and to wherever men gather and settle.

"The terminal depot. Why, it becomes real important. It becomes so important it brings out the greed in men. The original buyers, who often get the townships for a song, or a few cartwheels, start hauling in the money as other greedy men come west and start buying up the town lots. Look at the reasons why. When you have trade, and the rails bring trade, then you have to build hotels and houses for the traders, the teamsters, the hunters, the adventurers, the gamblers, the shopkeepers, the whiskey peddlers.

"And then you get the camp-followers, the loafers, the ne'er-do-wells, the soiled doves, the drifters and dreamers fleeing from Eastern towns following a path, landing on the new towns as if they dropped from the skies, like birds.

"The terminal depot becomes the center of a boom that lasts only for a while. As soon as the terminal depot moves forward, the people left behind must tap their own resources in order to survive. If the district has good advantages, it will stay there, thrive. If there is nothing of value to keep the village alive, it will die and the town lots will fall drastically in price."

Cheyenne had thrived, grown. And the town had sprung up almost by accident, so the story went. When the Union Pacific built westward, laying its lines, they put up a major depot, a division point, every seventy miles or so. These depots would have repair shops for the rolling stock. One was needed at the base of the Rockies and the U.P. had decided to call it Cheyenne. The surveying party rode ahead, trying to find a suitable site for the division point. Grenville Dodge, who had been a general in the Civil War, was the railroad's field boss. The party rode all day without finding a spot that suited all the needs for such a division point. Finally, as the sun was beginning to set, Dodge reined up, saddle-weary, and climbed down. He buried a hatchet in the ground and said, "By God, Cheyenne will be right *here!*"

Remington had seen the towns come and go, had seen them turn mild or ugly. Even back in Missouri, you could follow the tracks and there would be towns where, ordinarily, no towns should be. If the trains ever stopped running, he thought, the towns would die.

Cheyenne seemed destined to live on, but he was beginning to see its ugly underpinnings. Ultimately, even the best towns survived only because of its people and its laws. In a territory, like Wyoming, laws were often bent to suit its ruling class, and in Cheyenne, the cattlemen were kings. They commanded more land, more territory, and more votes.

Remington had no illusions about his job in Cheyenne. He was there to arrest a man on a federal warrant. But he was also there to see that no other federal laws had been broken. With Judge Barnstall's broad powers, the jurist had the power to see to it that the territories obeyed the law. And the U.S. marshals were at his beck and call. If Owen Carberry was protecting someone, or breaking the law, Remington had superiority over local concerns. If he had to arrest Carberry, he would.

Thus far, he had no evidence that Owen Carberry had broken any laws. But the man knew more than he was telling, and it appeared that in the past he had broken the law. If he had dealt in slavery, then he had something to account for. Harry Bellows had, it appeared, stumbled onto something far more insidious than cattle rustling. And, at the center, was Jack Cardiff, a man who sold his gun to the highest bidder.

Weary, Remington turned away from the window, walked to his bunk. He nodded to Weede, who was still poring over his notes, and lay down. He closed his eyes, tried not to think of all the things he had to do. He felt like a blind man groping in the dark. Worse, he felt that his hands were bound up and could not touch anything.

The marshal slept, but his dreams wore him out. They were full of fire and the sound of warning klaxons, and he was a man trapped and hindered from escaping the ravaging flames, the shadows of men with guns.

The three marshals rode out early, heading north from Cheyenne. Quail piped in the draws, and prairie chickens scattered through the grasses as they rode the rutted road, following a route they had learned from maps. The sun climbed high, burned off the dew, and they saw antelope on the far horizon, white and brown, motionless as stone.

They stopped for lunch in a clump of cottonwoods growing along Lodgepole Creek and watched the magpies flit through the leaves, drink at the stream. Tracks of deer laced the soft mud on the dry islands, and prairie swifts flew overhead in pairs, darting through the air as if on some desperate mission.

Weede sat propped against a cottonwood trunk, rifling through a sheaf of papers, making notes in a small lined tablet. Every so often, he would look off into the distance as if trying to think of something, but he did not say anything. Once, he caught Ned's eye, by accident. His dark face broke open in a wry, quizzical smile.

"You make any sense out your notes?" Remington asked, his face dappled by leaf shadows.

Weede grunted and shook his head.

Bucky swatted at a cloud of gray deerflies clustered on his trouser leg.

"Another ten, twelve mile," he said. "Be midafternoon before we get to Delaney's place."

"I reckon," said Remington. The horses stood hipshot in the shade, the last of the noon grain in their bellies. It would have been nice to just lie there in the shade and sleep, but he knew they had to get on. They had seen cattle for the past several miles, but no riders. Everything seemed peaceful, but this was only an illusion borne of endless prairie vistas and acres of blue sky and lazy white clouds drifting like ships toward the southern horizon.

"Let's ride," Remington said, forcing himself to his feet. He took a last swig of water from his canteen, slung it over his saddlehorn. "Keep a sharp lookout from here on," he said, stepping into the stirrup.

The three lawmen rode through the early afternoon, wider apart now, Weede and Kermit flanking Remington, who took the middle of the road. The cattle herds got bigger as they rode deeper into the country. They saw distant riders on the rolling swells, but could not distinguish their identity or the brand they rode for.

The road forked and a sign stood at the crossing. A thin 1 X 3 cut like an arrow was painted with the name DELANEY. This one pointed right. Another, with the name PHIPPS on it pointed left. Remington swung into the right fork as the sun started its downward arc toward the western horizon.

Three miles further on, the three riders passed under a wooden gate that was still under construction.

"Looks like Delaney means to make his mark," said Bucky.

Remington said nothing. He watched the skyline, saw the silver flashes. At first he thought it might be the sun glinting off metal, but the flashing continued.

"They know we're here," he told his deputies. "Riders are using hand mirrors to signal our approach."

"I see 'em," said Weede.

Bucky nodded, for he, too, had seen the flashing

mirrors. He reached in his pocket, pulled out two wads of cotton, stuffed them in his ears.

Remington smiled. Bucky's ears were delicate. If he thought there was a chance of gunplay, and if he had the time, he always put cotton wads in his ears. Weede checked his rifle in its scabbard, slid it up and down, left it in the boot, loosely.

They round wound through the low rolling hills, avoiding the worst of the washes and gullies. As they topped a rise, three riders came toward them, rifles across their pommels. Remington scanned their faces, did not recognize any of them.

The riders stopped, blocking the road. Beyond, Ned saw the tops of ranch buildings. Cattle grazed the rich grass; a few stood around a stock pond, the surface ruffled by vagrant breezes.

The marshals continued toward the three men who rode for the brand. They did not step up their pace, nor slow it.

"Steady now," said Remington softly.

"They look plumb primed," said Bucky.

Remington reined up a good fifteen yards from the middle rider, who seemed to be the leader. The other two men flanked him but were a few paces further back. There was no humor in any of the faces. These were serious men and they looked born to the saddle.

"That's far enough," said the man in the middle. He did not move his rifle, but the barrel rested lightly on the pommel and his right hand gripped the receiver, his finger inside the trigger guard. It was a Winchester '73, and the man looked like he knew how to use it. The hammer was cocked, and Ned had no doubt that there was a loaded cartridge in the chamber.

"We want no trouble," said Remington evenly. "But we're riding through."

"Not here you ain't," said the lead rider.

"We're United States marshals conducting federal business," said Remington. He flicked open his vest, displayed his badge.

"That badge don't mean nothin' out here," said the man. "We use 'em to scratch our asses."

Remington's jawline went hard, and his eyes flickered with a warning, but he took a breath and waited for his anger to cool.

When he finally spoke, he picked his words carefully and delivered them in flat, clear tones.

"Clear off this road and let us pass," Ned told the man. "I won't tell you again."

"Mister, this is private property and I'm sayin' you ain't goin' one cussed inch further."

Remington exchanged looks with his deputies. If it was to be here, on this ground, on this day, he thought, then let it be. The lead rider for the Delaney brand sat his horse like a stone, and it was clear he wasn't going to let them pass without a fight.

Remington looked him over, sizing him up. The man wore two days of beard stubble, a faded blue bandanna around his neck. His face was leathered from wind and sun, his eyes a stony blue. He had a small, pinched nose, thin lips that curled cruelly above a sharp chin. He wore leather chaps, carried a coiled lariat on his saddle. His pistol sat high in the holster on his gunbelt. The other two men looked every bit as determined as their leader. They were short, young fellows, with not a trace of fear in their faces.

"What's your name, mister?" Remington asked politely.

"What business is it of yours?"

"I always like to know the name of a man I aim to kill," said Remington.

Chapter Ten

A deadly silence sprang up among the six men. One of the young riders licked his lips, leaving not a trace of saliva. The other swallowed hard and his Adam's apple bobbed in his throat. The three marshals sat perfectly still, their eyes narrowed to slits.

Remington knew that what a man said could sometimes shift the balance. He had picked up the brand rider's challenge and thrown down one of his own. A smart man would figure that either the odds were even or they weren't. Either way, he had to have the confidence in his own ability. If the rider felt he was cooler, faster, truer in his aim, then he might think he had the edge. The rifle, loaded and cocked as it was, gave him a distinct advantage. That is, he might be able to get off the first shot. Maybe even another, before any of the marshals could draw a pistol.

But that was disregarding all of the unknown factors. Standing toe to toe, the rifleman might have the scales tipped in his favor in the first two or three seconds. But what if Remington or his men didn't sit still? What if they did something unexpected?

Remington knew that these things were going through the other men's minds as well. The silence stretched, tautened like a piano wire under strain. All six men were juggling information, assessing the facts, determining the odds.

In the silence, lives hung in the balance. A move, right or wrong, once taken, could not be canceled.

"My name's Ballard, you sonofabitch," said the middle rider and he brought his rifle up off the pommel, started to swing the barrel towards Remington.

As soon as Ballard opened his mouth, Ned knew what was coming. He did not wait. The brand rider was committed, the ball was open. Remington's hand streaked for his pistol. He rammed the rowels of his spurs into his horse's flanks, bent forward in the saddle. His hand closed around the plowhandle grip of his .44, jerked the pistol free of the holster. The weapon made no more than a soft whisper as it cleared leather. Ned's thumb forced the hammer back to full cock as the horse bolted toward the man with the rifle.

Bucky and Jimson hauled hard on their reins as they pulled away from Ned. Their hands clawed for sidearms as their horses wheeled, kicking up clouds of dust from the road. The other two Delaney riders brought their rifles up, but each move was two-handed. They were rooted in place as if their horses had grown out of the ground. They could not maneuver, they could not run, nor avoid the charging marshals. They could not hide.

Ned's horse raced straight for Ballard. Remington brought his pistol level as he ducked behind his horse's head and neck. He pointed the barrel, with its blade front sight, straight at Ballard's head and squeezed the trigger, allowing for his forward momentum. The pistol exploded, bucked in his hand. Ned cocked again and the cylinder spun.

Ballard fired, but his shot was not true. Remington

heard the lead ball sizzle past his ear, sounding like a hornet. He rode right into Ballard's horse, even as a black hole appeared just above the bridge of the rifleman's nose. Ballard opened his mouth to scream, but a sliver of bone sheared off into his brain. He crumpled like a strawless scarecrow and fell from his horse.

Bucky picked his man, fired through the dust as the kid tried to hold his rifle on Kermit. Bucky heard a cry of pain, saw the kid twist in the saddle. The rifle flew out of his hands, hit on its butt, clattered to the ground. Bucky fired again as the kid dug for his pistol. He saw the youth twitch and kick out of the saddle, a blood-spurting hole in his neck.

Jimson Weede followed Ned's tactics and charged his man, firing at point-blank range. The heavy Colt boomed and lead thudded into the young rider's side. He groaned in pain, fired his rifle so close to Jim's face that powder seared him, burned into his skin. Jim put two more bullets in the kid before he slumped over the saddle. His horse whirled to shake off the dead weight and the boy was hurled to the ground, dead in the air.

Jim hauled in on the reins, wheeled his mount. Smoke curled from the barrel of his Colt. The serpentine coil blew away in the wind, mixed with the scattered dust of the killing ground. The black man looked at the three riders, sprawled dead in blood-smeared grasses. His dark eyes clouded over with a sudden film.

"Dumb bastards," he muttered.

Kermit drew a breath, held his horse steady. His pistol still smoked in his hand and his eyes flared with the excitement of the battle.

Ned Remington slowly turned his horse, rode back

to where Ballard's body lay on its back. He looked down at the glazed eyes, the vacancy in them—for all time now, for eternity. The fight had lasted less than twenty seconds, and three men lay dead on the prairie, the high plains grasses waving gently in the breeze.

A moment's mindless thought, he mused, and an eternity to regret it.

Anger surged in Ned's blood, boiled in his brain. He cracked the gate on his pistol's cylinder, rammed the empty hulls out, let the brass fall to the ground. He shoved fresh shells in the empty tubes and snapped the gate shut. He thrust the pistol back in its holster, his eyes pale and shimmering with a steely rage.

Mirror flashes danced on the far rolling hills, sparkled like oversized fireflies in the searing daylight of afternoon. The news would reach Delaney before they got to his ranch. Remington didn't care. He was angry that three men had to die like this, so quick, so final, without saying any prayer. They died of arrogance and stupidity, he thought. They died for thirty a month and found, plus a bonus, he imagined, if they brought the marshals in toes down.

"Let's load 'em up," Ned gruffed.

"You goin' to ride in on Delaney packin' these jaspers?" asked Bucky, a querulous tone in his voice.

"He sent 'em out to bring us in the same way," said Remington.

"Damn right," said Weede, and Remington's anger cooled when he saw look of intensity on the black marshal's face.

"We'll go with rifles ready," said Remington, a bitter edge to his voice. "If anyone so much as twitches or blinks an eye, shoot to kill."

"Jesus," breathed Bucky. "This is getting serious."

"Damn right," Weede said again.

Remington laughed. These boys would do to ride the river with, he thought. These boys would do just fine.

John Delaney stood on the porch of the ranch house, feet spread apart, coatless and hatless. He was a pale-fleshed man with almost delicate features. His nose was thin and long, his lips pooched together in a perpetual pout. Yet, there was a hardness to his mien if one looked past his boyish features, into his steely-blue eyes, at the crow's tracks that framed them, at the streaks of gray in his thinning hair. He was not tall, but he gave the impression of height and strength. His Colt jutted from a holster worn high on his gunbelt. Four other men stood back of the hitchrail, each one holding a rifle. The flashing mirrors had told him some of the story, not all of it.

"Here they come," said one of the men at the hitchrail.

Delaney squinted, saw the silhouettes of the three riders as they topped the hill above the ranch house. They were leading three horses and the saddles were humped with the bodies of three of his men. Three good men. He knew their mounts, knew now what the mirror signals meant. Trouble, and then some.

Delaney turned toward the door, called to someone inside the house.

"Frank," he said. "They're here."

Frank Carberry stepped to the door, looked up the hill.

"All right," he said. "Might as well get it over with. Tell your men to put those damned rifles down."

Delaney's face flushed. He was not used to taking orders.

"Gary," called Delaney to one of the men out front, "put your rifles in a handy place and just hold steady. We don't want any trouble right off."

"All right, Boss," said Gary Winder. He spoke to the other three men. They walked around the side of the house, leaned their rifles against the shaded wall. In the corral, a horse whickered. Flies buzzed. A lizard slid out from the shadow of a rock, blinked in the sunlight, retreated. A crow cawed somewhere beyond the back pasture and buzzards circled a water hole a few miles away, riding the air currents, seldom flexing their wings.

Winder moved back toward the porch, leaned against the flooring.

"Never thought I'd see Ballard come in like that," he said.

"He was just too cocky," said Delaney, but his anger showed on his face. His throat was still scarlet from being ordered around by Frank Carberry. Things were not going well, despite Frank's assurances. U.S. marshals now. It made a man edgy, nervous. Poking around, looking under rocks. Frank had wanted to get it over with, meet Remington face to face. Ballard was Delaney's idea. Ballard was all for it. Too cocky. Yes. Sometimes a man lived a while longer if he was a little bit afraid. Trouble with Ballard was that he thought he was braver than any one else. He was brave all right. And now he was dead.

Delaney walked down the steps as the trio of riders pulling their gruesome cargo came closer. They passed the stock trough, turned into the lane that led to the house.

"Want me to walk out with you, Boss?" asked Winder.

"No, you just stay put, Gary."

"They're carryin' rifles."

"I see that. Just stay out of it until I tell you different."

"You're the boss," said Winder. Delaney wondered if he just imagined the sarcasm or if Winder knew things had changed.

Delaney saw the rifles. The men at the side of the house stayed close to their own weapons. It was possible there could be more gunplay. Delaney hoped not. He tried to imagine how it would turn out. Four against three. Five against three. Maybe six, if Carberry got into it. He wouldn't.

Delaney kept his hands away from his body. He wanted no mistakes.

The chief marshal reined up. His rifle bore dipped, aimed straight at Delaney.

"Marshal," said the rancher.

"John Delaney?"

"I'm Delaney."

"These are your men, I believe. They jumped us. Had to kill 'em."

"I'm right sorry."

"You put 'em up to it?" Remington asked. His rifle did not waver.

"No. They had orders to keep trespassers off my range land."

"They threw down on us, without provocation."

"Like I said, I'm sorry. Those two boys weren't dry behind the ears yet."

"They were big enough to shoot a rifle."

"Set down, Marshal. Frank Carberry's inside. We have some questions we'd like to ask."

"I have some for you and Carberry as well," said the lawman.

"Gary, see to our dead, will you?" asked Delaney. He did not look at the dead men anymore. His jaw hardened as he watched the three marshals set down. He looked at Weede a long time. The four hands began untying the ropes that lashed the dead men to the saddles. They carried Ballard off first, lay him out in the back pasture. The marshals followed Delaney into the house. Frank Carberry stepped forward as the lawmen entered the front room.

"I'm Frank Carberry," he said.

"Last time I saw you," said Remington, "you were catching a train."

"With Jack Cardiff," said Bucky.

"Sit down, gentlemen, won't you?" Carberry said politely. "I'm sure John wouldn't mind."

Delaney shot Carberry a look, then shrugged.

"We'll stand," said Remington. "We just want to ask you both a few questions."

"And then you'll be on your way?" asked Carberry.

"That depends on the answers," Ned told him. Carberry resembled his brother slightly. The facial structure was the same, but Frank's features were darker, his hair oilier, better groomed. He wore a business suit, a string tie, no handgun that Remington could see. He looked to be a few years older then Owen. He was almost as light-skinned as Delaney, but his was the flesh of a man who lived most of his life indoors. His nails were neatly trimmed, his sideburns cut precisely square, his hair cropped close all around. He was turning paunchy around the middle, but he was still trim for his age, which Remington took to be around forty-five or so.

Delaney stood by the fireplace. Carberry took a large easy chair, sat down as if he hadn't a care in the world. He crossed his legs, which furthered the illusion. The room, Ned noticed, did not show a woman's touch. There were no flowers, nor doilies on the modest, functional furniture. There was a divan, a big one, a low table, two easy chairs, one a Chesterfield, a small rolltop desk. Branding irons, spurs, bits, and other ranching accoutrements adorned the walls. There were antelope, buffalo, and wolf heads on the walls, as well, but no prints or samplers. In one corner, a glass-enclosed gunrack displayed a brace of sporting rifles, a Winchester '73, a Sharps .50, and a Kentucky muzzleloader with a curly maple stock.

"Carberry, Delaney," Remington said, "I'm looking for a man named Jack Cardiff. Do you know where I might find him?"

"I do not," said Carberry flatly.

"Me neither," said Delaney.

"You left Springfield with Cardiff," said the marshal.

"I did. We rode to Cheyenne together. I haven't seen him since."

"But you knew him before?"

"Yes. He worked for me some time ago, and I understand he was working for the Cheyenne Cattleman's Association."

"He's not working for them now?"

"I believe the Association has disbanded," said Carberry.

"Yeah, it broke up," said Delaney.

"You two rode in yesterday with a man named Morty Rittenhouse who works for you, Delaney. You walked up to the building that housed the Association's offices. Did you set the building afire?"

"No, we did not," said Carberry. Delaney shook his head.

"Did Rittenhouse?" pressed Remington.

Carberry shrugged. Delaney shot him a glance.

"John and I went to Delmonico's to talk some business," said Carberry. "Morty did not accompany us."

"Where is Rittenhouse now?" asked Remington.

"Why he's . . ." Delaney started to say. He stopped, looked beyond Remington, Weede, and Kermit, his eyes wide.

"Shut up, John!" barked a voice from the front doorway.

Remington turned quickly, saw the man with the double-barreled, sawed-off shotgun, standing there. His eyes were glazed, red-rimmed. Both hammers of the shotgun were cocked. He had the look of a madman. Both of his hands were swathed in grimy bandages.

"That's Morty Rittenhouse," said Carberry softly.

Weede and Kermit turned too.

The three marshals looked into the twin barrels, vacant and dark as a snake's eyes.

Rittenhouse's finger, jutting from the bandage, curled around one of the triggers.

Remington saw the madness flare in Morty's eyes as his glance swept the room. He swayed on his feet and the marshal could smell his alcohol-soaked breath from four feet away. He looked again at the twin snouts of the sawed-off shotgun, a deadly weapon at such close range.

He looked into Morty's eyes and knew that all of them were a trigger's pull away from death.

Chapter Eleven

Rittenhouse blinked, swayed there in the door-way. He refocused his eyes.

Sweat broke out on Delaney's forehead.

"For God's sake, Morty, go on back to the bunk-house."

"You tryin' to throw me to the wolves, ain't ye, John?" Morty's speech was slurred. "I heard ye talk-in'."

"Put the shotgun down," said Remington.

Morty laughed, shoved the barrels two inches closer to Ned's face. Ned did not flinch nor retreat. Delaney's lips began to quiver.

"I'm gonna kill John Delaney," said Rittenhouse. "And, you too, Frank Carberry. You bastards."

"Morty, calm down," said Carberry. Remington could give him that. The man was cool. Morty swung the shotgun away from Remington, pointed it toward Carberry in the chair.

That's when Ned made his move. He dove at the armed man, slashed a fist downward. He hammered into the wounded hand that held the shotgun. Morty screamed. The shotgun slithered from his grasp. Weede and Kermit jumped back as if struck at by a rattlesnake as the shotgun bounced around, its barrel spinning wildly. It crashed to the floor, jiggled for a few seconds, and then was still.

"Christ," said Bucky.

Rittenhouse staggered forward, lurched sideways, pitched past Remington toward Delaney. Delaney pulled his pistol and fired at point-blank range. The ball caught Rittenhouse in the chest. He went down to his knees, blood spurting from a hole in his back big enough to set a teacup in. Delaney took cold-eyed deliberate aim and shot him again, square in the middle of his chest.

Remington drew his pistol, took two quick strides toward Delaney and put the barrel to his head. He cocked the pistol.

"You shoot again and I'll blow your head off," said the marshal.

"He—he was comin' for me, damn you! I had to shoot him!"

"Bullshit," said Weede, looking at Delaney with dark contempt. "You killed that drunk in cold blood, man."

"You saw him, Marshal," said the rancher. "He—he was tryin' to kill me."

"Shut up, Delaney," said Remington, snatching the smoking pistol from the rancher's hand. "Sit down."

Delaney sat on the divan. His hands started shaking. Carberry sat calmly in the easy chair, his legs still crossed. He pulled out a cigar from his inside coat pocket, bit off the end. He struck a match, lit it.

Remington tossed Delaney's pistol to Bucky, knelt down beside the body of Rittenhouse. The segundo was dead, Ned knew, his heart blown to pulp. Bright red blood soaked the floor around him, but it had all come in a rush. The heart was no longer pumping.

Remington picked up one of the man's hands,

slipped off the bandage. He recoiled at the sight of the burned hands. The skin was gone, the raw flesh underneath lay exposed.

"This man's hands are burned," said Ned. "You know how it happened?"

"Morty fell into a branding fire," said Delaney.

"You brand this time of year?" Ned stood up.

"Sometimes. We've picked up a lot of strays, some we missed in spring roundup."

Remington strode to a spot in front of the divan. He looked down at Delaney with a pitiless stare.

"Mister," said Remington, "I think you're a damned liar. I think you're in this mess up to your armpits. I think you and Carberry meant to burn down the Cattleman's Association office and didn't care who you hurt doing it. I think you hired guns in town to kill Packer and Bradley, maybe me as well. I can't prove it right now, but I'm giving you fair warning. Federal laws have been broken. I'm here to uphold the law and to enforce it. Do you understand me?"

"Yes, Marshal, but I've done nothing illegal."

"You just killed an unarmed man. That's cause enough to take you in, bring you to trial."

"But—but he came in here armed. He was crazy. Drunk. He—he came for me. I had to shoot him."

"Delaney, Rittenhouse couldn't have killed a fly with those hands. You shot him in cold blood. I'm not going to take you in now, but I am going to swear out a warrant for your arrest. If you're still here when I take Cardiff, you're going back to Galena, Missouri in irons. You'll stand trial in Judge Sam Barnstall's court, and I'll be a witness against you. So will my deputies here."

"You're just tryin' to scare me. I know my rights. Frank here will testify that it was self-defense."

Remington swung around to look at Carberry.

"Carberry," he said, "if you say that, I'll call you a liar in open court."

"Marshal, you're making a lot of smoke," replied Carberry. "I don't believe you have any jurisdiction here. I haven't seen a warrant and I don't believe there's been one issued."

"I have warrants," said Remington coldly. "All I have to do is put names on them."

Carberry scowled.

"I've broken no laws," he said.

"Aiding and abetting a fugitive," said Remington. "Harboring a fugitive."

"Cardiff? You can't prove that."

"We'll see," said the marshal. "The same warning goes for you, Carberry. If you're still here when I take Cardiff, you'll go back to Missouri to stand trial."

Remington didn't wait for a reply. He strode to the door, followed by Weede and Kermit. Outside, he looked at the hands gathered around the front porch. No one spoke. Remington and his men mounted their horses.

"Is that all?" asked Weede. "Seems to me you had cause to put both those men under lock and key."

"I want the word to get around," said Remington. "I *am* making smoke."

"Cardiff?"

"Yes. I want him real bad, Jim."

Remington clapped spurs to his horse's flanks, rode back the way they came. Later, Bucky caught up to him.

"Where to now, Ned? We going to see Phipps?"

"No. Let's see who comes down this road and where they go. I imagine Phipps will get the word soon enough."

"I see what you mean."

They rode to the crossroads, went a short distance beyond. Remington looked around for suitable cover, found a place where they could hide the horses and look down at the road from a low hill some distance away. They groundtied their horses in a gully, crawled to the crest of the hill, lay in the tall grasses, their rifles ready just in case there was trouble.

Fifteen minutes later, two riders appeared on the horizon. As they approached, Remington saw that Delaney and Carberry were not sparing their horses. When the two men reached the crossroads, they did not turn toward the Phipps ranch, but continued on, south.

"Jimson, let me see that map we made again," said Remington. Weede dug the map out of his pocket, handed it to Ned. He studied it carefully. In the distance, he saw Carberry and Delaney leave the road, ride off to the west.

"Interesting," he said.

"What do you make of it?" asked Bucky.

"We may have been barking up the wrong tree," said Remington. "Or missing one. Maybe not a tree, but a sprig."

"What do you mean?" asked Weede.

"We've been looking at the big ranchers," Ned replied, "those who are fighting over the water along the Lodgepole. What about the little fellers? What do they stand to gain? How can they survive?"

"What're you sayin', Ned?" asked Bucky, shoving his hat back off his forehead. The two riders disappeared in the distance. A frail line of dust hung in the air, marking their route.

"I'm not sure I've got it all straight yet, but I think we need to worry over it some before we go on. I've got Harry's notebook in my saddlebags. Jimson, you've got your notations taken at the courthouse, still."

"Right."

"Let's go back to the horses, do some looking and thinking."

"I wish somebody would tell me what's going on," said Bucky, a tone of exasperation in his voice.

"Pretty quick, Bucky," said Remington, with a grin. "As soon as we know."

The three men walked back down into the gully. Kermit rolled a smoke as Weede fished papers out of his saddlebag. Ned unwrapped Harry's daybook, found a flat rock to sit on and stretched out his long legs. He opened the book, listened to the rattle of papers as Weede went through his notes. Bucky paced back and forth, drawing smoke into his lungs, spewing it out in long, blue flumes.

A passage in the daybook caught Ned's attention. It was one he had read before, but it was the writing after it which fascinated him: "Rustlers gone. No arrests. J. Cardif had bill of sale for cattle. Bought from Faron. Case closed. Maybe." The "Maybe" still bothered Ned. He read on: "Cardif worked for Banse. Banse worked for Packer. Found C Bar P cattle cold-branded. Suspect Banse built herd from rebranded beeves."

Remington looked up from the daybook.

"Bucky," he said, "Know anything about cold-branding?"

Bucky laughed. "I've seen it done," he said. "It's mighty bold. Risky."

Weede set aside his papers for a moment. "What's this cold-branding?" he asked.

"Feller rides for the brand," said Kermit, "and wants to build him a little herd, he can do it real easy. He gets him a sack, wets it down good. He puts the sack over the calf's hide, runs the brand on top of it. The branding iron burns off the hair underneath, but don't go down to the hide."

"I don't get it," said Weede.

Remington chuckled. "The owner looks at the calves, sees that his brand is there," he said, "and forgets all about it. Later on, the hair grows back over the temporary marks. The cowhand comes back later, burns his own brand into the hide. This time he does it straight and the brand is burned in deep, permanent and there isn't a trace of the earlier marking."

"Pretty slick," said Jimson.

"Yeah," said Remington, "and Harry thought maybe Faron Banse was doing some of this when he worked for Packer."

"He worked for Packer?" asked Weede. "That's funny."

"Why?"

"He was one of the smallest ranchers hereabouts. Now, from these records I jotted down, he seems to have done pretty well."

"In a short time?" asked Kermit.

"In a short time," said Weede.

"What are you saying?" asked Remington.

"I'm saying that a man who was one of the smallest ranchers in the Cheyenne Cattleman's Association is now one of the biggest. But he did it on the quiet, according to the records I looked at."

"Maybe you'd better explain," said Ned.

Weede grabbed up a bunch of papers, looked at his notes. He cleared his throat, wiped a line of sweat from his brow.

"He first filed on a hunnert and sixty acres, back about three years ago. Little piece of land on the Lodgepole. Then he bought another chunk from a sodbuster. That doubled his land holdings. After that, he bought more land from guess who."

"Jack Cardiff," said Remington.

"That's right. And Cardiff got the land from settlers who signed over to him."

"So, what do we have?" asked Remington.

"We've got a little man who's now a big man and still growing, with a land- and water-hungry herd," replied Weede. "And his property drives a wedge between Phipps and Delaney, butts up to Packer. Looks to me like he's got to get more river property if he's going to survive. Right now, according to the plat maps, he's got a checkerboard of land that scoots in and out of land held by those three other ranchers."

Kermit let out a low whistle.

"What else do we know about Banse?" Bucky asked.

"Not much," said Remington. "But Harry was somewhat suspicious of him. Now, it appears that his suspicions were well-found."

"So, what next?" asked Weede.

"I think we've been looking for Cardiff in the wrong places. Banse seems to be pretty smart. Tricky, I mean. It could be that he bought Cardiff off, lured him away from Carberry and his bunch. Maybe with the promise of land, maybe as a full partner. One thing sure; Banse couldn't have done it alone."

"I wonder why Packer and the others never tumbled to it?" asked Bucky.

Ned looked at the two deputies, his mind racing. Just beyond his grasp was the final answer. It was like something that crawled out of a bog in his mind, but was still covered with mud. He could see its outline, but not its true shape. He had to clean it off, examine it. His brain clawed at it, tried to grasp it, but the thing kept slithering away.

Somewhere, back of all the shenanigans, behind all the land grabbing, the rustling, the slave labor, the killing, there was a common denominator, someone who knew all the answers, who either took part in the whole scheme, very quietly and very unobtrusively, or who engineered it from a distance. There was someone in the background who was able to hide the true facts of what was going on from some of the participants, from the Cattleman's Association itself.

It probably wasn't Packer. Delaney, maybe, or Phipps. But Remington eliminated those. The one who knew the whole scheme wasn't someone so actively involved as any of those ranchers. But it was someone who knew them all, knew what they were doing and probably saw an opportunity to feather his own nest. To find that man, that someone who protected the guilty, he'd have to go through a process of elimination.

"We've got to ask ourselves some hard questions," said Remington. "I think we can find the answer if we work it through among ourselves."

"All right," said Bucky. "What are we looking for?"

"One man," said Remington. "At the center. He probably isn't a rancher, but he could be. He's someone who's watched all this going on and maybe looked the other way, or worked with different ranchers at different times, pitting one against another until a time when he could step in and take it all for himself."

"Jesus," exclaimed Bucky, "that man would have to be pretty smart. Pretty cool, too."

"Yes," said Ned. "Now, let's go through the names. We've got Packer, Delaney, Banse, Morriss, Phipps, Cardiff, the Carberrys."

"Delaney?" suggested Weede. "Maybe Phipps, too?"

"I don't think so," Ned said softly. "Delaney is in trouble. I think Frank Carberry came up here to find out what's going on. I think Delaney's desperate. He knows something's wrong, but he doesn't know what."

"Could be," said Weede. "He's heavily mortgaged. Phipps, too."

"Who holds the mortgage?" asked Remington.

Weede's eyes widened.

"Damn!" he exclaimed. "I almost missed it. I just never connected the name until now, until just this minute."

"Well, don't keep it a damned secret," said Bucky, sarcastically.

"Yeah," said Remington. "We'd like to know."

Before Weede could reply, four rifles cracked from the ridge above them. They looked up, saw the spouts of orange flames. Heard the crack and whine of bullets spanging off stone. The three marshals dove for cover, pulled pistols from leather holsters.

Men appeared on the skyline, hunched over in the tall grass. They fired again and moved in closer, sure of their prey.

Remington hunkered behind a rock, looked at the

opposite slope. There was no way out. They were trapped in the gully and outnumbered. He drew his pistol, but he knew before he even cocked it that the range was too great.

It was a hell of a way to die.

Chapter Twelve

The riflemen slid through the tall gamma grass, set up firing positions. The three marshals had little or no chance to get out of the gully alive, unless they could find cover, reach their rifles. The men on the ridge were shooting from a hundred and fifty yards.

Ned looked up at the afternoon sky. There was still plenty of light left. He doubted if they could last until dark. He looked at Weede, who rolled behind a small rock. Bucky crawled backward into a clump of bushes. The horses stamped their hooves and rattled their reins, trying to shake loose from their moorings.

It was a hell of a situation.

"Hold your fire," said Remington. "Stay down."

"We're in a bad spot," said Bucky softly. "I can't even see them up there until they shoot."

"I know," said Remington. "We can get out of this if we keep our wits."

"How?" asked Weede.

A shot cracked on the slope above them and a bullet plowed a furrow through the grasses. The bullet smashed into rock, sprayed Weede with grit.

Another shot spattered Remington as it flayed the earth a few feet from his head. Bucky winced as the bushes rattled with still another shot.

"They're not trying to kill us," said Remington. "Why?"

"Look!" said Weede, pointing up the draw.

A man carrying a torch ran along the mouth of the gully, setting the grasses aflame.

"Over there!" shouted Bucky.

Remington looked in the other direction, saw a man at the head of the draw doing the same thing. Flames crackled as the dry grass caught fire. Fanned by the wind, the fire traveled quickly, burrowing down into the gully where the three marshals lay trapped. Ned turned over, looked up the slope. Two men ran along the ridge touching burning torches to the tinder-dry grasses.

The horses screamed as smoke assailed their nostrils.

The rifle fire kept them pinned down. Choking smoke blew down the draw as the flames leaped higher.

"They're tryin' to burn us alive!" shouted Bucky.

Remington knew the plan now. No bullet holes in them. No marks. They would be burned to death in a range fire. Common enough in cattle country. Most anything could set dry brush or grass afire in the dry part of the summer: a match, a carelessly tossed cigarette, a spark, lightning. No one would ever know.

"We've got to get to the rifles," said Remington. "Bucky, you and Jimson, cover me."

The rifles lay near the pile of papers and Harry's daybook they had abandoned when the firing broke out. Ten feet away, but right out in the open. Ned knew he would expose himself to withering fire once he moved, but without the long range weapons they were as good as dead. He fired his pistol at the last flash of orange he saw, then scrambled to his feet. He began running toward the rifles.

Bucky and Jimson began firing their pistols, aiming high, hoping their bullets would carry three hundred yards up the steep slope of the gully.

Remington dove as the rifles just below the ridge began to bark. He hit the ground, rolled quickly as geysers of dirt and grass and stone spouted up all around him. He slid quickly, grasped the butt of his own rifle. He rolled again, cocking the Winchester while on his back. He flipped over onto his belly, scooted up to a rock.

A volley of rifle fire pinned the chief marshal down. He closed his eyes to keep from being blinded by grit. The firing died away and he started scanning the slope for a target. He saw a man raise his head and, allowing for bullet drop and gravity, took aim, squeezed the trigger.

He heard a far-off cry, saw the bushwhacker throw up his arms, fall into the grass. Seconds later, the man rolled down the slope, his companions firing through the smoke. Remington crawled over to the other rifles. He picked up Bucky's, called to him.

"Here you go, Bucky!" Ned hefted the rifle, threw it like a spear to Kermit. Bucky caught it deftly, grinned. "Jimson. Catch!" Remington tossed Weede's rifle to him, arcing it high. A volley of shots kicked up dust spouts all around them. Weede caught the rifle, holstered his pistol.

"Pour it into them," ordered Remington, "and start moving back toward the horses."

"Okay," yelled Weede, taking aim at a man on the hillside.

Bucky shot one of the men carrying a torch. It took him two shots to bring him down, but the man screamed and fell into a burning patch of brush. Remington looked up the slope, saw a man kneeling, taking aim. He brought his rifle to bear, quickly figured trajectory and windage, fired. He saw the man topple, grab his leg.

"Just a mite off," he said to Bucky, who grinned wide.

"I'll get him," said Kermit, and did just that.

Remington started to slide backwards, toward the horses. He took a circuitous path, picking his shots carefully. The men with the torches threw them down and began firing down into the gully. There were only four left, Ned figured. But they were shooting, not to kill, but to keep them trapped. He and his men had no such good intentions.

"Lay it into them!" Remington shouted, scooting backwards.

Smoke billowed down into the gully. Suddenly, Ned realized that the smoke might turn out to be their salvation. If the horses didn't bolt, they had a chance. He saw Weede move backwards, duck-walking, firing, rolling away, firing again.

A wall of fire began to form around one end of the draw, burn down toward the bottom of the gully. At the other end, the wind blew the fire back towards the top. Ned saw a man running along the rim and he fired off a shot to discourage him. The man threw down his firebrand and ran over the rim, disappeared.

Weede reached the horses first, got behind them.

"Steady, now," he said to the gelding he had rented. He caught up the reins of the other two mounts. "Come on Ned, Bucky. We can ride out of here."

"Let's go," said Remington. He got to his feet, ran a zigzag pattern toward the horses. Bucky covered him with fire until his hammer clicked on an empty chamber. He got up, ran the short distance to the horses, got on the other side where Ned and Jimson waited. He dug into his saddle bags for more ammunition, began shoving them into the magazine chamber.

"We've cut 'em down some," he panted. Remington and Weede reloaded their rifles.

Up on the hill the firing died down.

"Something's up," said Weede.

Remington nodded.

"Listen," said Bucky, cocking a fresh shell into the firing chamber of his rifle.

They listened, heard the distant sound of rifle fire. Pop, pop, pop, like Chinese firecrackers. They heard closer rifle fire, up on the other side of the ridge.

"Come on," said Remington. "We'll never get a better chance than this."

The three lawmen mounted their horses, followed Ned as he raced up the slope where the fire had not spread. No rifleman blocked their progress. They crisscrossed the slope, rested the horses just below the rim. The horses panted from the exertion. Their hides glistened in the afternoon sun, slick with sweat. Tendrils of dark smoke smudged the horizon around the gully rim and wisps of it blew toward them on the breeze.

They topped the ridge, saw the dark clump of riders chasing those who had been firing down into the gully. They rode back toward the Delaney spread. Eight or ten horsemen pursued them, firing like cavalrymen from their horses. Remington and his deputies watched the uneven fight for several seconds, giving their mounts wind. One of the pursuing riders saw them, turned away from the pack, headed their way. Others broke off, in singles and twos and raced after them.

"Who do you figure we owe for this?" asked Weede.

"Jesse Packer, I'd say."

"That looks like Brad coming right behind him," said Bucky, his keen eyes slitted against the slanting rays of the sun.

"Let's ride out and meet them," said Remington. "Take it slow and be on guard."

Moments later, they met Packer on the plain. Bradley rode up shortly afterward, breathing hard. The two men looked at the burning prairie, the curtain of smoke that hung in the sky.

"Looks like you've been busy, Remington," said Packer.

"Those Delaney's men who jumped us?" he asked.

"Right. We were checking our stock, heard the gunfire, came running. When we saw the smoke, we figured they were up to no good. That's my land they set on fire."

"Why were you checking your stock?" asked Remington.

Brad and Jesse exchanged glances. Their faces darkened as if a shadow had passed over them.

"One of my line riders spotted some men driving off cattle late this morning. He's pretty sure one of them was Jack Cardiff."

"Did they get away?" asked Bucky.

"They did. My rider was outgunned. They got thirty head, near as I can figure."

"Know where they went?" asked Weede.

"Headed southwest," said Brad.

The firing stopped, and the remaining Packer

riders began to stream back toward Remington and the others.

"That would be Banse's lands, wouldn't it?" asked Remington.

"Why, yes," said Packer. "But Faron Banse. Hell, he's . . ."

"He's what?" asked Remington.

"Why, he don't need my cattle. He's just a small rancher. Got more stock now than he knows what to do with."

Remington sat silent on his horse, looking directly into Packer's eyes. Packer's lips compressed. He ran his tongue over his lips.

"Banse?" he said tightly.

"Maybe," said Remington. "He's not so little anymore. Fact is, he stands to gain more than any of you if you get to fighting among yourselves."

"Faron? He's just a pipsqueak," said Brad. "Small in both mind and body."

"Sometimes you have to watch those little ones," said Remington. "They can get some big ideas."

"I see what you mean," said Packer. "But I would never figure Faron for a rustler."

"I think that's how he got started. Know anything about him?"

"No, not much. He come up from Texas, worked for me and for Delaney, or Phipps. I can't remember. He got him a small spread, bought some calves. Built him a nice little herd, but he's way off from the rest of us."

"He's been slowly acquiring more and more land," said Remington. "Jimson, what's that you were going to tell us before we got jumped."

"Yeah," said Weede, "you were asking about who held the mortgage on Delaney's property. The deeds show the name of an outfit called Washington Holding Company."

"Why—why, that's the company that holds the mortgage on my property," said Packer. "It was recommended by the Cattleman's Association. Two percent interest. Best we could get. Whole bunch of us got money from 'em to keep going when the rustling got so bad."

"Doesn't that name mean anything to you, Packer?" asked Remington.

"No. Why should it. I gather it has some national meaning. George Washington, maybe."

"No," said Remington softly. "Amos Washington. And, Amos Washington was owned by Frank Carberry. Maybe Owen Carberry as well."

"We—I never did know who owned the company. The papers all came through the Association and the Bank of Laramie. The money was good."

"Might be a lot of strings attached to it," said Ned.

"Owen Carberry? No. He never had anything to do with the Association," said Packer.

"Maybe," said Remington. "Who started it?"

"Why, all of us did," replied Packer.

"John Delaney came up with the idea," said Bradley.

Remington raked both men with a scathing look.

"And Frank Carberry tells Delaney when to jump, fart, scratch, and buy beans," said Remington.

The look on their faces told the lawman that he had struck bone.

Chapter Thirteen

For a long time no one spoke. Packer's men shifted uneasily on their horses. Jesse looked at Bradley as if he had been kicked in the groin. Brad looked down at the ground.

"Men, get your blankets and start putting out that damned fire," Packer barked. "What in hell do you think this is? A picnic?"

Sheepishly, his men rode off toward the prairie fire which was largely contained in the gully. They stripped their horses and began to beat out the flames along the rim. Bradley and Packer stayed, each locked into his own thoughts.

"What can we do?" asked Packer.

"I'm going to ride over to Banse's," said Remington. "I have a hunch we'll find Cardiff there. You can go on about your business, or I can deputize you."

"We want to come along," said Packer. "Brad?"

"Count me in."

"Jimson, swear them in," said Remington, turning his horse. He stopped, waited for Weede to finish. He checked his pistol and rifle, slapped dust off his clothes. He was ready. Weede's revelation had made sense of a lot of things that he hadn't understood be-

fore. Behind it all was a single man, Owen Carberry.
He was quite sure now that Frank answered to him.

It seemed only logical, now that he thought about
it. Owen was the town marshal of Cheyenne. As
such, he had considerable power. Also, he was the
man closest to the problems of the ranchers and
settlers. He was the one called in to settle disputes.
He would know the weaknesses of each man. His
brother Frank was probably the money man, the fi-
nancier. So, the two had cooked up a scheme to bring
about a bloody range war and create a mortgage company that would be sitting pretty when the dust settled.

It was neat and ugly at the same time. Everyone
seemed to trust Owen Carberry. Of course. He was
The Law. He was the Keeper of the Peace. But his
background showed different. He was a slaver who
didn't let the war's end stop him. Amos Washington
and the other blacks had been tricked into working for
the Carberrys, at slave wages. Out in the West, there
would be few questions asked. The slavery question
had very little effect on those living in Wyoming Territory. And Owen had kept it quiet. So far as anyone
knew, Amos and his confreres were freed slaves who
came out West to work cattle.

But Remington knew differently now. Harry Bellows had stumbled onto it, but he had been killed
before he could make sense of his notes. Amos Washington had probably been marked for death. Ned
would bet a month's pay that Amos's name was on
the Washington Holding Company records as founder
and president. A perfect scheme, except Amos knew
that his life would not be worth much once the Carberrys achieved their goal—to have the biggest cattle
ranch in the territory and no one to challenge them.

Bold, yes, and daring. Illegal as hell, too, if you cut into the bark and found the worms underneath.

Harry had made the first slash, the poor bastard. Now, the peeling.

"Jim," said Remington. "Let's get our papers out of that gully. I want Harry's daybook. It might be evidence."

"I'll get the stuff," said Weede. "I've ate smoke before."

Remington watched the black man ride off. He had a great deal of respect for Weede. The man did his job. He never talked about the past in ways that some men did. He never brought up his color, even when others did, and he didn't back off when called out.

Ned was glad he had brought Jimson along. He hoped it was for the right reasons. Weede would know, when it was all over. Remington knew now that it wasn't just because Amos Washington was a black man, but because of Harry Bellows. Harry hated men who thought they were superior because of their race—whether they were white, black, red, or the color of sand. Bellows took a man for what he was inside, not how he looked on the outside.

"Guts are the same, blood is the same," Harry told Ned once. "Indians bleed same as whites. Niggers, too. I've seen good men and bad, but it wasn't the color of their skins what made 'em diff'rent. Ned, I tell you, true. Sometimes I get skin as black as any African, and more'n one time I been as red as a Mescalero Apache."

Remington drew a deep breath. He could almost feel Harry's presence as he and the others moved across the rolling country, heading for a rendezvous with a man who might prove the most dangerous of all—Faron Banse. In Ned's book there was nothing worse than a sneak. And, from all he'd learned and surmised about Banse, he was a man cut from the same mold as the Carberrys. He kept to the shadows. He presented one face, but lived behind another.

Weede caught up to the other four riders a half hour later. He patted his saddlebags to show Ned he had gotten the papers and Harry's daybook.

"How far?" Bucky asked, after an hour's ride.

"Five more miles," said Packer.

The men rode grimly on, and the tension began to build. There was not a man among them who did not know they were heading for a showdown. None of them knew what to expect, but they all knew that their lives were on the line.

The afternoon shadows stretched long over the sage as the five riders topped the last hill on the Quarter Circle B Ranch. They looked down at the ranch house, the several outbuildings, including bunkhouse, barn, stables, blacksmith shop, and cookhouse.

"Faron has growed some," remarked Brad drily.

In a corral behind the main house, men ran cattle through a chute. A fire blazed, and men looked up at the approaching riders. One of them held a running iron in his hand.

"Those your cattle?" asked Remington.

Packer shrugged.

"We'll find out," said Remington, touching spurs to his horse's flanks. They rode at full gallop toward the back corral, saw the men—most of them black— scatter, climb through the fence. Ned drew his rifle from its scabbard and the others did the same.

One of the men in the corral stood his ground. He was bigger than the others and he carried a fifty-caliber Sharps. Remington looked at him very closely. His heart began to pound hard enough to make his ears ring. His pulse raced with excitement.

"Hey," yelled Bucky into the wind, "that there's Jack Cardiff standin' all by his lonesome in the corral."

A small man stepped out onto the porch. He wore a pistol high on his hip. He shaded his eyes against the setting sun, looked at the oncoming riders.

"That's Faron Banse on the porch," said Packer.

"Fan out," said Remington. "Shoot if you have to."

The five men spread out, but no one fired at them. Men ran to the bunkhouse and the cook looked out of the cookhouse, then slammed the door. He, too, was a black man.

Jack Cardiff stood his ground, his rifle cradled in his arms. He did not bring it to his shoulder.

Remington rode straight for the corral. Weede closed the gap, came up alongside. Bucky rode to the bunkhouse, Bradley with him. Packer rode toward the house, rifle in hand.

The riders reined up, trained rifles on the men they could see.

Remington walked his horse to a spot some twenty yards from where Cardiff stood, his feet widespread, his look defiant. The man was huge. Everything about him seemed oversized: his hands, his feet, his head, his neck. The Sharps looked like a toy in his hands. His black hair swept back from a large flat forehead. Cardiff's nose brooded like a granite sculpture over thick, fleshy lips. He stood six foot five, Ned figured, in his stockings.

He leveled the Winchester at the giant man, cocked a shell into the chamber.

"You gonna shoot me, Marshal?" Cardiff mocked.

"Not unless you move real sudden," Ned replied.

"I'm thinkin' real hard about it."

Cardiff's eyes flicked as he looked at Jimson Weede. He scowled.

"It would be over mighty quick," said Remington.

"Better'n hangin'."

"Maybe."

"What do you want?" asked Cardiff.

"I'm arresting you for the murders of Amos Washington and Harry Bellows," said Remington. "Drop your rifle and put up your hands."

Ned wondered, even as he spoke the necessary words, if it was going to be that easy. Cardiff showed no sign that he was ready to surrender his Sharps. Instead, he held it across his chest like a sword, defiantly, as if daring someone to take it from him. Ned felt his anger rise, just looking at the rifle. He knew that it had been used to kill his friend, Harry, and a black man who only wanted to run away from trouble.

"Can't we talk about it some?" asked Cardiff.

"Nothing to talk about. I've got a warrant for your arrest."

"Your word against mine."

"We have an eyewitness," said Remington, nodding in the direction of Bucky Kermit.

Cardiff looked at Bucky. Recognition seemed to wash over the giant man's face.

"Now, I want you to put your rifle down and step back five paces," said Remington. "Put your hands up high, over your head, and just stand steady."

Weede poked his rifle toward Cardiff in a gesture urging the big man to make haste. Cardiff set the Sharps down, took five paces backward. He raised his hands over his head, palms out, stood there. Remington shoved his rifle in the boot, drew his pistol. He dismounted, walked through the open corral gate toward Cardiff.

Remington drew close. Then, he stopped dead in his tracks. He never saw a man move so fast. Cardiff took a long step and threw himself on the ground. His hands grasped the Sharps, brought it up to his shoulder. Remington, caught offguard, broke into a run. He counted seconds that stretched into eternity as he dashed across an interminable distance.

The explosion almost burst his eardrums, but he knocked the rifle aside and clubbed downward with the butt of his pistol. He heard the butt strike the top of Cardiff's head, felt the crunch of bone. The Sharps skidded in the dirt. Cardiff, shaking off the blow to his head, lurched to his knees. Remington swung the pistol again, cracked it off the giant's jaw. Cardiff slammed a hard fist into Remington's side. Ned felt the wind go out of him and saw the corral spin wildly about him, blur as he staggered sideways.

Cardiff stood up, towered over Remington. He swayed for a moment, steadied. He came toward the marshal, fists cocked like a pugilist's. He swung his left and Ned heard the air swish as if a sudden wind had sprung up. He ducked under it, saw the right coming at him with tremendous speed. He bent over, heard the mighty fist pass over his head with an ominous hissing sound.

Remington kicked upward, aiming for the Goliath's groin. He rammed his boot into Cardiff's testicles, heard the man grunt with pain. Remington pushed hard with his boot, saw the giant topple, go down. Cardiff hit the ground on his back and the earth shook with the force of his weight.

Remington dropped on top of Cardiff with one knee. He drove the knee hard against the outlaw's chest. Then, he rammed his pistol barrel against Cardiff's forehead, cocked it. Cardiff's dark eyes widened.

"One move, one twitch, Cardiff, and I'll blow your brains to mush," said Remington tightly.

Cardiff lay frozen on the ground.

Remington felt the hatred boil up in him again. He slid the barrel of the pistol down alongside Cardiff's nose, pried up his mouth. He shoved the barrel down the big man's throat. His finger curled around the trigger.

Cardiff gagged.

Remington drew a breath. His finger began to quiver slightly, eased toward the curved metal trigger. He felt a rough hand on his shoulder.

"Ned, leave him be," said a soft, gravelly voice.

Ned looked up, saw Jim Weede standing over him, his face dark against the blue of the sky.

"Goddamn him, Jim," said Remington. "Goddamn him to hell."

"You can't do it, Ned. Let me take over."

Weede put his hand on Ned's wrist, closed around it. He withdrew the pistol barrel from Cardiff's mouth, gently pushed Remington away. Cardiff spluttered, sucked in air. Remington stood up, covered the giant man as Weede poked the outlaw with his rifle barrel.

"It's all over, Cardiff," said Jimson. "I'm arresting you for murder."

"No nigger's taking me in!" snarled the killer.

"That's right," said Weede. "But I am. And I'm a deputy United States marshal."

Cardiff looked pleadingly at Remington.

"You take me in, Marshal. I don't want no nigger doin' it."

Remington looked at Cardiff with disgust.

"Jim," he said to Weede, "if this nigger gives you any trouble, kill him."

Jimson Weede grinned wide.

Chapter Fourteen

Jesse Packer glared at Faron Banse as the fight in the corral ended. Both men watched as Jim Weede prodded Cardiff toward the house at the end of a rifle barrel. Cardiff's hands were tied tightly behind him with leather thongs.

"It's all over, Faron," said Packer. "Drop your gunbelt and step down off that porch."

Banse, a small man with a crisp, thin moustache, sunken, close-set feral eyes, feminine lips, frowned as he saw the other deputy empty the bunkhouse at gunpoint. The black men emerged first, with hands folded over the tops of their heads, followed by three white men who came out into the sunlight as meekly as their dark brethren.

"Get off my land," said Banse.

"I'm arresting you, Faron," said Payne.

"You can't arrest me, Jesse."

"Yes he can," said Bradley. "Me, too. We've both been deputized by the marshals here."

"Why, you sonsofbitches," spat Banse. He started to go for his pistol, but Bradley fired a round into the porch next to Faron's feet. Banse halted his movement, glared at the two men. He touched the buckle on his gunbelt, but he did not unbuckle it.

"What are you arresting me for?" he asked.

"Rustling," snapped Packer, his anger flaring. "Looks to me like we caught you dead to rights."

"Looks you been doin' it a long time, Faron," said Bradley. "Marshals there got evidence enough to hang you."

Banse's face clouded up. Suddenly, he drew his pistol, cocked it. Packer started to fire, but Banse brought the pistol up to his temple. He squeezed the trigger. A flash of orange flame, a puff of smoke, and his brains spattered the wall of the house. Faron's legs crumpled and he went down, a lifeless rag doll that sprawled over the edge of the porch, his skull dripping blood and fluids onto the ground below.

"Christ," said Bradley.

"I didn't think he'd have the guts."

Remington and the others approached and looked at the dead man. The blacks murmured among themselves. The white men turned away in disgust. One of them got sick and vomited all over himself.

"Some of you men take those stolen cattle back to Packer's spread," Remington announced. "There won't be any charges if you carry out my order."

The hands nodded and ran off with alacrity.

"What now?" asked Packer.

"We'll take Cardiff in, lock him up. You and Bradley are free to go. We can handle it from here on out."

"What about Carberry and Delaney? They might still cause you trouble."

"We'll worry about that when the time comes. I'll have a talk with Owen Carberry when we get to town."

"Be careful going back." The rancher clapped

spurs to his horse. "Much obliged, Marshal," said Packer. "I'll help run those cattle back to my ranch."

"Thanks for your help," said Remington.

Kermit brought up a horse for Cardiff and Weede got the prisoner mounted. The marshals rode off, Remington in the lead, Weede and Kermit flanking Jack Cardiff.

Before they had ridden a mile, Cardiff began taunting Jimson Weede.

"You think you're a free nigger, don't you?" he asked Weede.

"I was manumitted before the war," said Jim easily.

"Hell, we used to find 'em hiding in the cellars, drag 'em out and sell 'em again," said Cardiff. "We loved seein' the free niggers come over the border into Missouri. They said they was free, but we'd ask 'em, 'Where you gonna go, boy? Back to Africa? To Liberia? You can't go there. You can't go to Honduras or Nicaragua even if you had boat fare.' So, they'd look real puzzled and we'd chain 'em up and sell 'em. We sold 'em to Injuns, whites, didn't make no difference."

"War's over," said Bucky, irritated at Cardiff's vicious banter. "No more slaves."

"Haw!" exclaimed Cardiff. "Them black boys back there. You think they're free? Banse owned 'em, lock, stock and barrel. They run off, I'd kill 'em."

"Like you did Amos Washington?" asked Weede.

"'Zackly. That no-account nigger thought he could outrun me."

"Cardiff," said Jim, "you're a bastard."

"Naw, I got me folks," taunted the prisoner. "I bet you don't even know who your mam and pap were."

"Shut up, Cardiff," said Bucky.

"Ain't that right, nigger?" Cardiff wouldn't shut up.

Weede said nothing, but he closed his eyes and opened them again. They burned with something inside him, some long ago hurt that hadn't healed over.

"Look at him," said Cardiff, "tryin' to act white. That badge don't change your color, son. Your peoples got more troubles now than they had before the war, before that dunce Lincoln emancipated y'all. You'll always be suckin' hind tit like your black brothers. Second-class trash."

"You sonofabitch!" spat Bucky. "If you don't shut up, I'm going to ram my rifle barrel down your gullet."

"Haw! The nigger knows I'm right. Hell, you can't stop a man from talkin', sayin' what's true. Ask the nigger if he ever sets down with whites at table and eats chicken with 'em. Go ahead, ask him."

"Jim can sit at my table any time he wants," said Bucky.

"But I bet he never has," retorted the prisoner.

Bucky and Weede exchanged sad glances. Weede grinned. Bucky's eyelids knotted with rage and frustration. His hand fisted his reins, gripped them tightly. Cardiff chuckled to himself.

Remington halted, turned his horse, rode back to the three men.

"What's all the arguing about?" he asked.

"Cardiff's climbing Jim's back about his color," said Bucky.

Remington pierced Cardiff with a searing glance.

"Cardiff, you keep your mouth shut. Jim Weede's a deputy United States marshal and you'll treat him with respect."

"He ain't fit to shine my boots," said Cardiff.

"I'll have him kick your ass with *his* boots if you give me any more guff, mister."

Remington seethed inside. Some men, he knew, just couldn't forget that the war was over. Men like Cardiff were the worst kind. They knew how to gouge the wounds, make a man like Weede feel like less than a man. But, he wasn't about to succeed with Jimson. Jim had won his own freedom and he never was a lackey. He was a man. Remington knew that Cardiff's words must sting him, nevertheless. Words could hurt.

Remington had thought about this happening when he had chosen to bring Weede along. A black man had been killed. Someone had to speak up for that man, right or wrong. He didn't know if Amos Washington was a lawbreaker or not. He didn't care. He had been murdered, and that was not only against the law, but against every moral principle Remington believed in. Cardiff had to answer for that crime. He would answer for it, in a court of law. Judge Barnstall's court.

"You lockin' me up in Cheyenne?" asked Cardiff, as Remington turned his horse, rode back up front to take the point.

"I am," said Remington.

"Owen will never let you take me back to Missouri."

Remington reined up, suddenly angry again.

He let the others catch up as he cooled. When they did, he turned his horse, looked Cardiff square in the eye.

"You mind explaining that, Cardiff?" asked the head marshal.

"Naw. Me'n Owen go back a long ways. We was

slavers together before the war and during it. Him and his brother Frank won't let you get out of Cheyenne alive."

"You seem pretty sure of yourself, Cardiff," said Remington.

"You don't believe me? Look!"

Cardiff hunched forward, nodded his head. Remington turned around. Bucky and Jim looked down the road. A line of men sat their horses, blocking the road to Cheyenne. Remington counted them. Four, five, six, seven, ten men with rifles pointed straight up in the air waited for them. There was no mistaking their purpose.

"Looks like trouble," said Bucky.

"That's Delaney and Frank Carberry," said Weede.

"Three to one," said Kermit.

The riders were some four or five hundred yards off. Remington knew he had to make a decision. If they wanted Cardiff, they'd have to pay dearly for him. But he didn't want that. Now that the man was his prisoner, Ned was responsible for his well-being. He had to protect him as well as he did his own men. That was part of his job.

"Looks like you lose," said Cardiff, tauntingly. "That's Charlie Phipps with 'em, and his bunch are hard players."

"The game hasn't even opened yet," said Remington, off-handedly.

"You can bet they didn't come to talk," Cardiff pointed out.

"Bucky," said Remington. "Next time Cardiff opens his mouth, you shut it for him. We can take him across the saddle as well as sitting up straight."

"Right, Ned," said Bucky with a wide grin. "It

would give me great pleasure to crack this bastard's head open."

Cardiff sulked, but he kept his mouth buttoned.

Remington turned his horse, rode over beside Jim Weede.

"What do you think, Jim? We could try and ride around them, maybe flank them. Or, we could ride right over them, shooting on the run. Or, we could turn around and go back, defend ourselves from the Banse House."

"For a while, yes. They'd burn us out, or starve us out," said the black marshal.

"Flank?"

"No. We'd tire the horses before we ever got off a shot."

"My thinking too. What, then?"

"Ride right over them," grinned Weede. "They're in our road."

"Damned right," said Remington, smiling. "Slow or fast?"

"Slow. We've got a prisoner to protect."

Ned slapped Jim on the back.

"That's just what I wanted to hear," he said. "Come on, Bucky. Let's ride."

Bucky prodded the prisoner in the back.

"You lie flat over that saddle, Cardiff," he said. "You so much as raise your head and I'll put a lump on big as a gooseneck squash."

Remington kicked heels into his horse's flanks, charged. He felt the animal's haunches bunch up as he broke into a run, then into a full gallop. The wind tore at his face. He drew his pistol, hunched over. Behind him he heard the thunder of hoofbeats as the other horses galloped after him. He looked at the line of men ahead, saw them bring their rifles down, then lift them to their shoulders.

He would not encumber himself with the rifle. Let the Delaney and Phipps bunch shoot at moving targets, at long range. By the time their rifles were empty, Remington would be right on top of them. He began turning his horse slightly, setting up a zigzag pattern.

Orange blossoms of flame, followed by puffs of white smoke sprouted from the distant rifles. Ned heard bullets fry the air, whine as they struck stone and caromed off fifty yards ahead of them.

The rifles boomed and cracked. Remington knew they were trying to find the range. He hauled his horse hard over, then back again. He left the road, came back to it again. Pop, pop, pop, pop, the rifles cracked and bullets whistled past them. The rifle fire increased and the distance closed between the charging riders and those sitting still two hundred yards ahead, now a hundred, and then fifty.

Remington picked a target, fired at thirty yards. He saw the man spin in the saddle, like a top, and then pitch from his horse to land facedown in the dirt. He fired again, striking a horse, and behind him he heard Weede and Kermit open the ball with their own six-guns.

The riders bolted and raced around in confusion. Some tried to reload, but their bucking horses made it impossible. He saw a man go down under Weede's pistol and Delaney, screaming something he couldn't hear, rocked back on his saddle as Bucky's bullet caught him in the gut.

Smoke and the smell of gunpowder filled the air.

"Kill Cardiff!" yelled Frank Carberry. "Kill him!"

Remington saw Carberry turn his horse and try to

run away. Frank threw his empty rifle over his shoulder. Remington took aim at the horse's rump and fired from ten feet away. It was like taking a running buffalo. The horse's hind legs sagged for a moment, then crumpled. Frank flew off the horse like a scarecrow caught in a whirlwind. He hit the ground with a *whump*, the breath knocked out of his lungs.

"They're ridin' off!" yelled Bucky.

"Let 'em go," said Weede, firing at the retreating riders.

Cardiff, still slumped over his saddle, bristled with anger as Bucky led him up to where Frank Carberry lay sprawled on the ground trying to draw in a breath.

"I heard you, Frank," said the prisoner. "You traitorous sonofabitch."

Remington wheeled his mount, halted so that his horse threw a shadow over Frank Carberry. He aimed his pistol at Frank's head.

"Get up," he ordered, "real slow. I'm arresting you for interfering with a federal officer in the performance of his duties."

"I wouldn't do that if I were you," boomed a voice from close at hand.

The marshals looked up.

Owen Carberry and two deputy city marshals sat on their horses, rifles leveled at the federal lawmen. They had come up so silently, no one had heard them in the excitement.

"Aren't you out of your jurisdiction?" asked Remington coolly.

"Maybe. I don't know how to figure boundaries. There's trouble, I come to it."

"I'm arresting your brother," said Remington.

"No, you ain't, Remington. Not without a warrant."

"I've got one. One for you, as well."

"You'll never serve 'em," said Owen.

He cocked the hammer back on his rifle, brought it up level to Remington's head.

Time seemed to freeze. The sun held tight on the western rim of the land forever. The long shadows stopped in their tracks.

Remington stared grimly into the eye of Death itself.

And he was not afraid.

Chapter Fifteen

At that moment, Jack Cardiff sat up straight in his saddle. Owen Carberry looked toward the movement for a fraction of a second.

Sometimes entire histories are written in a split second. One moment a man is alive and the air sweet in his lungs. The next, he is looking into the face of eternity, looking at the last thing he will ever see on this earth. All of the years before seem wiped out in that last flash of light before darkness comes. Histories are written and settled. Eras come to an end. Lawlessness is erased from one corner of the land.

It was that way with Owen Carberry and his two deputies.

In that tiniest fraction of time when everything in the universe is still, three rifles barked and three saddles emptied. Owen flinched as Weede's bullet caught him above the belt buckle. The rifle dropped from his hands as if it was a chunk of iron plucked from a blacksmith's forge. Bucky shot a deputy at point-blank range. Ned took the other one out, no questions asked.

Three men twitched and kicked on the ground. Each was alive. Each was bleeding.

Remington swung out of the saddle, kicked rifles

out of his way as he squatted beside Owen Carberry. Bucky jumped off his horse and threw down on Frank Carberry who tried to crawl to his brother's side.

"Hold it right there, Frank."

"My brother . . ."

"He got what he came for," said Bucky coldly.

Cardiff looked on with glazed, lifeless eyes.

Remington took Owen's pistol out of his holster, stuck it in his belt.

"It's all over, Carberry," he said.

"Yeah. I—I figured."

"He told us you was breakin' the law," said one of Owen's deputies. "We didn't think there'd be gunning."

"Your mistake," said Remington.

Owen groaned and grabbed his belly with one hand. Blood soaked over his fingers. He looked down, saw the crimson pump of blood from his stomach.

"I'd like a smoke," he said grimly. "Guess I can't have a drink of water."

"You haven't got a hell of a lot of time, Carberry," said Remington, fishing in his pocket for the makings. "But I'll roll you one."

"Thanks. It could have worked, you know."

"No, I don't. You were wrong from the start."

"I had it all worked out. Frank and me."

"You got off on the wrong foot," said Ned. "Slaves. It was bad from the beginning."

"Yeah, I think you're right." He watched with glittering eyes as Remington rolled his last cigarette, pouring the tobacco from the sack of Durham onto the crimped paper, squeezing it shut like the mouth of a purse. Ned onehanded it, licked the rolled quirly, pinched the ends shut by twisting them. He stuck the quirly in his mouth, found a sulphur match, struck it. He held the match to the cigarette, puffed on it. He handed the smoke to Carberry, who set it shakily between his lips.

The town marshal drew deeply on the smoke and choked. His face contorted in pain. Blood gushed from the hole in his abdomen. His eyes began to glaze over with the agony coursing through his body.

Remington looked at him. It would not be long now.

"Me and Frank spent a long time settin' this up," said Owen, his voice slow, halting. "We brought in the Negroes and we made money on both ends. We bought good land cheap when the U.P. came in and we sold it dear. We didn't know cattle, so we—we started pickin' the men. It was like a card game. You watch faces, watch the way a man plays. You make a side bet, you bet on the player. Know what I mean?"

"Yeah," said Remington bitterly. "I put my money on Harry Bellows."

"Good man, Bellows. Smart. Maybe too smart."

"Why did you have to kill Amos Washington?" asked Remington.

"He—he knew it all. He wanted out. I thought he might shoot his mouth off like a two-dollar cannon. I always liked Amos. He—he helped us a lot with the Negroes."

"What about Cardiff? He was the wrong man to send. He made a big impression on eyewitnesses. Both when he killed Washington and when he killed Deputy Bellows."

"Jack? Why don't you ask him?"

"What is he?" asked Remington. "Your cousin? Your uncle? A shirttail relative?"

Carberry took another pull on his cigarette, tried to

laugh. The laugh set him to coughing and he lost more blood. His face began to slick with the sheen of sweat and Remington knew that he couldn't hold on much longer.

"Brother," he said. "Half-brother, really. When Pa died, Ma took up with Lucas Cardiff. Jack killed him when he turned fourteen. Luke beat the hell out of us, and Jack he stood up to him. Ma never forgave him though."

Remington sat back on his legs, rocked there for a moment. Suddenly a lot of things made sense. Cardiff looked more like Frank than Owen, but the resemblance was there. It was as if someone had cast the Carberrys into a bigger mold, added hate and prejudice and bigotry to an already sour creation.

"Let me see my brother," pleaded Frank Carberry. "Before it's too late."

Remington looked at Bucky, nodded. Bucky brought Frank over, kept him a yard away from his brother. Cardiff looked on with black slate eyes.

"Owen," said Jack, "you talk too damned much. Look how you got things all balled up."

"Jack, you're a sonofabitch," said Owen, his voice reduced to a raspy husk.

"I know," said Cardiff. "We both had the same worthless mammy."

Hatred flared in Owen Carberry's eyes. Frank looked at his brother with something like pity. But, the fear was there, too. Remington saw that Owen had probably had mixed feelings about Cardiff all these years. Liking him, maybe, and hating him at the same time. But, Owen was the smarter one, if intelligence counted.

"Owen, hold on," begged Frank. "Don't die. Please don't die."

"Frank, snivelin' ain't gonna help a whole lot," said Owen. He forced a grin. Frank's face turned waxen.

"You better save your strength," said Remington. "We might get you into town, to a doc."

"No, couldn't even set a horse," said Owen. "You take care of my deputies, though. They wasn't in on this whole thing."

"Did you really think you could make it work?" asked Ned. "Building something on a shaky foundation?"

"Yeah, I thought it would work. Would have if you hadn't come along. Frank said he could handle you. Jack, he just didn't watch his backtrail like I told him to."

Cardiff hawked up a gob of phlegm, spit it into the dirt. The horses moved restlessly, switched tails, whickered.

Owen's eyes glazed over and he shuddered with a sudden spasm of pain. Eternity was a lot closer, now. He knew that. He looked off at the sinking sun, at the western sky smeared with blood and ashes. It would be dark soon. Very dark. He took a last puff on the cigarette, handed what was left of it to Remington.

"I'll say good-bye to you, Frank," said Owen.

"What about me?" taunted Cardiff.

"You can go to hell," said Owen. "I'll be waitin' for you."

"Owen, they'll hang me, too," said Frank.

"Then we'll all meet there, by and by," said Owen.

Frank broke down then, started crying. He buried his face in his hands and the sobs shook his body. No one could look at him. No one could face a man crying like that, crying like a woman.

The sun sank over the mountains suddenly. The long shadows moved again, thickened.

Owen Carberry opened his mouth to say something, but no sound came out. He gurgled and something terrible rattled in his throat. He let out a short gasp, then slumped over. Remington put a hand to his neck, but felt no pulse.

"He's dead," he told Frank. Frank sobbed even louder.

Cardiff snorted.

Remington stood up. He kicked one of the deputies, who was only slightly wounded.

"Get him on a horse. We'll take him into town, see that he gets buried. Bucky, get Frank mounted. We've got some dark to go through before we get back. I don't want to risk being jumped out here again."

"Yeah," said Bucky.

"So long, you bastard," said Cardiff to his half-brother. "Keep the goddamned fires warm."

Remington watched the prairie stream by outside the smoke-smudged window of the train heading eastward. He listened to the clackety-clack of the iron wheels on the track. A few seats ahead of him sat Bucky and Frank Carberry. On the opposite side of the aisle, Cardiff was chained to the seat, Jimson Weede beside him, reading *The Cheyenne Leader*.

It was all over, maybe. Banse was dead, his ranch divided up among the surviving ranchers. Packer would reorganize the Cattleman's Association. One of the town deputies died the day after they brought Owen's body in, and the town council fired the other one.

Remington leafed through Harry Bellow's daybook. He had read the whole thing through the night before in the hotel room. Damn. He missed Harry. The daybook, though, would be important evidence in the trial of Jack Cardiff.

He almost laughed aloud now, thinking about that one passage he had perused long after midnight when he was sleepy, but still wound up over all that happened.

Harry had written: "Think Cardif might be blood kin to Carbery. Bigger, badder, stupider. Funny, if so. If I had a relative like Cardif I'd resign from the human race."

That was Harry, always making a joke. Even when things were blackest, he would come up with a crack that would make everyone laugh.

"Well, Harry," Remington thought, "you can laugh now. You showed us the way. We got your man."

Bucky turned around, looked at Remington.

"You talkin' to yourself, Ned?"

"I was just thinking about Harry Bellows."

"Me, too. What was you thinkin'?"

"A couple of things," said Ned. "One is that I think we avenged his death."

"And the other?"

"That dead men can tell tales."

"Huh? That don't make sense. Ned, you ought to get some shut-eye."

"It makes sense to me," said Ned. He lifted the daybook and held it up high.

Harry's Last Will and Testament.

And Justice for all.

CHANCE

The Maverick with the Winning Hand

**A blazing new series of Western excitement
featuring a high-rolling rogue
with a thirst for action!**

by Clay Tanner

CHANCE 75160-7/$2.50US/$3.50Can
Introducing Chance—a cool-headed, hot-
blooded winner.

CHANCE #2 75161-5/$2.50US/$3.50Can
Riverboat Rampage

CHANCE #3 75162-3/$2.50US/$3.50Can
Dead Man's Hand

CHANCE #4 75163-1/$2.50US/$3.50Can
Gambler's Revenge

CHANCE #5 75164-X/$2.50US/$3.50Can
Delta Raiders

CHANCE #6 75165-8/$2.50US/$3.50Can
Mississippi Rogue

CHANCE #7 75392-8/$2.50US/$3.50Can
Dakota Showdown

CLASSIC ADVENTURES FROM THE DAYS OF THE OLD WEST FROM AMERICA'S AUTHENTIC STORYTELLERS

NORMAN A. FOX

STRANGER FROM ARIZONA
70296-7/$2.75US/$3.75Can

THE TREMBLING HILLS
70299-1/$2.75US/$3.75 Can

LAURAN PAINE

SKYE   70186-3/$2.75US/$3.75Can

THE MARSHAL   70187-1/$2.50US/$3.50Can

T.V. OLSEN

KENO   75292-1/$2.75US/$3.95Can